Other Books by Randy Jurado Ertll

Hope in Times of Darkness: A Salvadoran American Experience

Esperanza en Tiempos de Oscuridad: La Experiencia de un Salvadoreño Americano

The Life of an Activist: In The Frontlines 24/7

In The Struggle: Chronicles

The Lives and Times of El Cipitío: La Vida y los Tiempos del Cipitío

The Adventures of El Cipitío: Las aventuras del Cipitío

LA SIGUANABA

AND

THE MAGICAL LOROCO

a novel by

Randy Jurado Ertll

Published in the United States of America by

ERTLL PUBLISHERS

www.randyjuradoertll.com

Cover illustration by Billy Burgos

ISBN 978-0-9909929-9-8 (pbk.)
ISBN 978-1-7342708-0-8 (ebk.)

First edition 2020

Printed in the United States of America

1 2 3 4 5 6 7 8 9 10

LA SIGUANABA

AND

THE MAGICAL LOROCO

CHAPTER 1

"These motherfuckers are gonna pay" said La Siguanaba. She was no longer a mojada from El Salvador. Now she had billetes. Puros dolares to buy anything and anyone that she wanted. She was the wealthiest Latina businesswoman in the Virginia, Maryland, District of Columbia D.C. *(DMV)* areas. She had mansions throughout the United States, and she lived part time in Los Angeles since she wanted to keep it real on the West Coast. She loved to blast NWA, Tupac, and Notorious B.I.G.

She was *la vergona* en los Estados Unidos. She was the *ovario* queen. She would tell her friends "hay que tener ovarios hijos de la gran puta."

During the day, she was a true mesmerizing beauty, but at night, when she would become enraged, she would show her true colors and horrific features. Her hair would become long as fuck, her nails would grow immensely razor sharp, her tits would expand and sag tremendously. She was constantly fighting her inner demons, but she had achieved amazing success in the United States. El sueño Americano.

She was la chingona. No one could fuck with her anymore. Her laundry business was making profits in the hundreds of millions per year. In the billions if you add all of her wealth and properties. She had sealed contracts with the Pentagon, to wash, fold, and press every single uniform from the Army, Navy, Marines, and Air Force. She was so tight with the Pentagon that she would invite Generals to eat nuegados con miel y chilate.

She had even fucked Donald Trump – to the point that she left him *todo jugado* y *baboso*. She would tell her comadres, "ese dundo tiene un pene chiquito, como una banana Chiquita. Nada de majoncho. You don't even want to know about La Siguanaba's affair with Melania. Their secret favorite song is *Love Of My Life* by Queen.

La Siguanaba only bought the very best perfumes, silk dresses, imported Italian shoes, and cheese from Winconsin. During her tea parties she would tell her guests "yo solo ordeno queso de Winconsin. Ese queso duro del Mercado Central huele a pura pata chuca."

Las demas señoras adineradas le decían "no jodas vos, lo compraste en el Mercado Cuartel — y se echaban las carcajadas que hasta se tiraban pedos."

After they would eat pupusas con café, at *Los Molcajetes* restaurant, and smoke marijuana joints for her arthritis — La Siguanaba would start to hallucinate and remember her fucking evil enemy — El Cadejo. That fucker had finessed La Siguanaba. She was currently reading Dale Carnegie's *How to Win Friends and Influence People* and watching reruns of Billy Graham's evangelical Christian sermons. She wanted to see if she could forgive and win over her enemies. She figured that if a cult leader and serial killer, Charles Manson read Dale Carnegie's book, then it must be hella good. She wanted to see if she could forgive her enemies by reading self-help literature. She detested El Cadejo with a passion.

That asshole, El Cadejo, would still haunt her thoughts and she wanted to read as many books as possible to forget her fragmented, broken past. She had all of the money in the world, but her heart still ached due to the brutalities that she had endured.

La Siguanaba no longer spoke to her two sons: *El Cipitio and El Duende*. They still resented her ass, especially *El Cipitio* since she had drowned him in *la quebrada* since he was a little three feet, pot belly, dark skin, little motherfucker, born with backward feet.

She was her own woman and did not need any fucking problems nor help from needy men. She birthed them and could destroy them if she wanted to. She would tell them "I brought you to this world and I can take you out, hijos de la gran puta!

CHAPTER 2

Her great nemesis was *el maje* known as El Cadejo. That motherfucker could take on any physical shape, but his true physical appearance was of a wolf like dog who could appear as a white or black image. His eyes were bright red as if fire were in them – the pits of hell. He could howl and whistle. He could hypnotize his prey. He had extraordinary strength and he was part of the undead since he inherited eternal life from the Prince of Darkness. He has existed for many centuries. It was rumored that the Prince of Darkness was the true owner and creator of El Cadejo. El padre del Cadejo era el mero diablo. No wonder he was fucking intensely evil and powerful. However, El Cadejo had a soft side and he could be kind at times. But this was hella rare.

Anytime anyone would whisper his name, El Cadejo, La Siguanaba would fly into a state of rage. She was doing everything in her power to control her satanic side and diabolic looks. She wanted to remain la señora hermosa y bien esculturada. Men would still salivate like dogs when they would see her. Puros perros calientes. She knew that they thought with their dicks and not with their brain. She knew she could get anything she wanted from them. She talked to them with her corazón and wore red g strings, with white pants and tight ass skirts, when she wanted to seduce them.

She would say to her herself, "estos cipotes cerotes cagados, ni me pueden satisfacer bien." She became so tired of penises, that she began to explore vaginas. She would hire the biggest asses to clean her mansions. She would begin to fantasize like Arnold Schwarzenegger - regarding screwing the *help*. She figured if men took advantage of the help/servants in El Salvador, Guatemala, Nicaragua, Honduras, y Mexico then she could do the same in *Los Uniteds*. She began to seduce other women by buying them luxurious gifts. She knew how to romance her next big conquest. She was *la bisexual*. One of her biggest well kept secrets was her romantic conquest of Melania Trump. She had met and screwed Donald Trump at Jeffrey Epstein's little sex island. Trump told Epstein "that bitch rocked my world a hundred times more than Stormy Daniels. That nance perfume drove me crazy. I want more of that pussy with loroco." The fool was sprung – estaba enculado. He had only met other Salvi women who were maids at his hotels and resorts and who had given him a pound of authentic Salvadoran *queso duro* as a gift to him for not reporting them to ICE (Homeland Security). They did not want to return or to be deported to their native country since women continue to be disrespected and exploited at all levels.

Many men in El Salvador are known to take advantage of the maids/servants. They called them in a derogatory manner "la muchacha" or "la servidumbre." Human rights and Civil Rights are non-existent for the working class in El Salvador/ Central America and Mexico. No matter what Lopez Obrador says, the indigenous are still treated as second class citizens in Mexico.

El Cipitio and El Duende thought they had successfully eradicated El Cadejo. They were wrong. El Cadejo continued to roam Central America, Mexico, United States and other parts of the world. El Cadejo's soul returned with a vengeance. That motherfucker could never die. Like he always would say while taking methamphetamine and crack hits — "we never die, we just multiply." He loved quoting *American Me*, the movie, by saying "somos pocos pero locos."

That fucker was boiled in holy water through a sopa de patas. However, a piece of his ear, the earlobe, was forgotten — and through the immortal genes from that little piece of ear — he came back to life. He wanted revenge just like La Siguanaba. He hated his two sons: El Cipitio and El Duende — who orchestrated the hit on him. He would mumble to himself "esos hijos de la gran puta me las van a pagar. Malditos." Then he would blast Iron Maiden's best hits to relax while he hit the crack pipa. The pipe. When he really wanted to feel gangster he would blast YG and he would wear a red shirt, a red beanie, red Nikes, and red underwear. He would jump into his red El Camino and he would blast "Who Do You Love?"

In order to continue fooling people, El Cadejo came up with an ingenious plan — he took on the physical appearance and persona of a Russian mobster. That fool learned Russian in a few days through The Rosetta Stone videos.

He even moved to Moscow to run Vladimir Putin's illicit business enterprises and money laundering bank schemes throughout the world. He took on the nickname of "The Bitch." He developed a deep understanding of Russian history and culture by purposely seeking to be imprisoned in a Gulag. Like the ones where Joseph Stalin would place all of his enemies. He became the leader of the Gulag political prisoners and hardened criminals. El Cadejo even infiltrated the NKVD — Russia's secret police. He wanted to immerse himself in the details of the Russian underworld. El Cadejo's nickname became known as El Zek or sometimes Semion. and he was quite proud of that shit. The motherfucker was so devious that he could take on any appearance that he wanted. El Cadejo had teleporting powers and he could time travel. El Cipitio inherited these supernatural traits from El Cadejo.

He could be white, black, or any color that he pleased, and he could take on any physical appearance that he wanted. Rumor circulated that he was born in a castle in a small village of Russia — centuries ago. Villagers still kept it quiet since they did not want the evil demon to return. El Cadejo roamed the forest of Siberia where he would attack and eat travelling humans. They were happy that he had migrated to Hungary where he became Count Dracul, he also lived in Spain and then deported to the Caribbean and eventually landed in El Salvador. Where the fuck do you think Bram Stoker got the Dracula idea from? Transylvania. Stoker simply expanded the Hungarian/ Romanian folklore stories regarding Count Dracul. He wrote and published his novel in 1897 — but the folklore of Dracula had already circulated for centuries.

AKA El Cadejo learned how to infiltrate and blackmail people through Putin's extensive experience in the KGB. He learned that purposely creating an enemy attack would help to create nationalism, a clear enemy, and an excuse to attack a foreign government. Planting bombs became one of his attributes. If a little country began to talk about independence or breaking away from the grip of Russia, all of a sudden they were accused of being terrorists and the Russian hammer would come down, hard. They were oppressed — just like under Stalin, Lenin, and Chairman Mao. Putin was the modern-day strong man — with billions of dollars and technology that would put the United States to shame. How the fuck do you think Hillary Clinton lost the election to Donald Trump? Social media infiltration and laser targeted messages.

The Russians are experts in creating rumors and it worked against Hillary Clinton. Ironically, her biggest Achilles heel was none other than Socialist Bernie Sanders. He looks like Mr. Furley from the hit television show *Three's Company*, but he is no bumbling fool. He took on the Democratic Party as a Socialist/Independent and he became a top contender for the U.S. presidency.

Sanders once lived as a single father in Vermont with no running water or electricity in his modest home. But he is now a multimillionaire and a true presidential contender. Esta cabron ese viejito. He would win if he were to join forces with Senator Elizabeth Warren. The Sanders/Warren ticket would automatically become the dynamic duo of politics. The Russians did meddle into the elections by buying millions of dollars in publicity and marketing through Facebook, Twitter, Instagram, and other social media platforms. Their messaging was masterful and voters throughout America believed them.

El Zek, originally known as El Cadejo, wore fancy watches, gold chains, drank excessive coffee, and drove a top of the line Mercedes Benz. His favorite coffee was Turkish and Armenian.

El Cadejo was so fucking evil that he was hired by the Ottoman Empire (Turkey) from 1915 to 1918 as a key consultant to assist in the development and implementation of the Armenian Genocide. The Committee of Union and Progress (Ittihad ve Terakki Jemiyeti) — known as the Young Turks. El Cadejo would drink Vodka and party with Mehmet Talaat (Minister of the Interior), Grand Vizir (Primer Minister), Ismail Enver (Minister of War), and Ahmed Jemal (Minister of the Marine and Military Governor of Syria). El Cadejo was given the contract to lead the Special Organization (Teshkilati Mahsusa) — to exterminate the Armenian population. Over 1.5 million Armenians were murdered from 1915 to 1918. El Cadejo was nicknamed the hoe ass rat by the Turks, since he had no morals or scruples, but he went by the official name of Behaeddin Shakir, a so-called doctor. He demanded to be addressed by The Doctor since that made him feel very important. He was proud of his expert consultant services in ethnic cleansing. To avoid prosecution of World War I (WWI) crimes against humanity El Cadejo fled to Spain, where he also became a close advisor to Spain's Franco. El Cadejo learned a lot of repressive tricks from Franco and he also served as a close advisor to General Martinez in El Salvador who had strong pro Franco and Nazi sympathies. El Cadejo was an elusive evil fucker that could take on various personas. He could possess someone else's body.

In modern days, El Cadejo became the top advisor to President Donald Trump. He told Donald Trump "I can get any shit you want from the Russians — Vodka, silk ties, submarines, Mercedes Benz at a 50% discount." Trump simply said to him "Fantastic, fabulous." El Cadejo also promised to be the best *infiltrador* to progressive movements. He discussed how progressives would want to unite under one common banner to oppose Trump and El Cadejo's thoughts were "fuck those motherfuckers, I will give them one bottle of Vodka and a $1 million grant and they will be happy as clams. That impeachment shit will go nowhere and will actually strengthen Trump's base of supporters."

El Cadejo became intrigued by Socialists Bernie Sanders, Elizabeth Warren, Kamala Harris, and Alexandria Ocasio-Cortez. He particularly liked Ocasio-Cortez since she knew how to dance, and she reminded him of Sarah Palin. He knew that Senator John McCain had chosen Palin as his running mate since he found her attractive and wanted to ultimately screw her. Self-interest does in fact reach the upper crust of power.

CHAPTER 3

L a Siguanaba was restless. She was tired of fucking anything and anyone she wanted. She acted just like Freddie Mercury, George Michael, and Elton John. She was pretty much Bill Clinton in his prime. She started to imagine herself as the first guanaca Pope of the Roman Catholic Church. She thought to herself, "I already have billions of dollars and men will do anything I order them to do. If I develop a strategy to become the first ever female Catholic Pope—I will be able to cook succulent pupusas en el Vaticano. She wanted the visitors to smell flores de loroco. Only organic ingredients. Con tierra natal. She loved the architecture and engineering of the Vatican. She was influenced by Frank Lloyd Wright's beautiful designs — especially his Mayan architectural accomplishments.

La Siguanaba had to develop a winning strategy. She figured you have to fight crazy with crazier. She would have to return to her *colonia* attitude and shit. The D.C. ghetto attitude. She had to prove that she had hood credentials. She was an undercover chola and she had to showcase that she was true pueblo — from the barrio. Just like la Jennie Rivera — from Playa Larga (Long Beach - The LBC) and Cardi B from the Bronx, Nueva York.

La Siguanaba wanted to be all fancy, but she came from a morbid, dark, world. She kept a deep secret that no one could know about. She had been kidnapped as a child and sold into the sex trafficking business. A coyote had convinced her mother and father to let him bring her to the United States. But it was a ruse, a set up. The coyote was a sex slave smuggler and he

11

would go to the small villages throughout Central America to recruit and kidnap small children. He would then sell the children to the Central American gangs and Mexican cartels. This was her biggest and most painful secret. She kept it so hidden in her subconscious that she led herself to believe that it never happened to her. She felt as if it was a nightmare that she'd had.

La Siguanaba had gone through unspeakable experiences in El Salvador where women are not respected but exploited. She lost touch with her twin sons El Cipitio and El Duende — who hated and resented her. They did not understand nor were they aware of what she had gone through in her tiny, native, heartless and cruel country. It is the world's most violent and dangerous country for women and children. Current president Nayib Bukele has taken a proactive approach to decrease the violence and to offer safety to the Salvadoran citizenry. Ese Palestino esta pesado y tiene pisto propio - asi que no tiene que hueviarle al pueblo.

Thousands of young girls and boys are choosing to commit suicide rather than to be raped, tortured, or murdered by the criminal gangs. Many girls who become pregnant because of the rapes eventually choose to commit suicide. This would enrage La Siguanaba who believed in abortion. She felt that women should have a choice and not be criminalized for choosing to have abortions. Many people in the United States continue to pretend that they do not comprehend nor understand why tens of thousands of children continue to migrate to the United States.

Trump referred to Central American countries as 'shithole countries' and he is aware that no one really cares nor understands why tens of thousands of children are literally walking and running for their lives to Mexico, the United, States, and Canada. Sadly, people are running for their lives because their home countries are inhabitable. They are escaping to survive and to save their lives. Many of these countries are going through tremendous climate change and water is no longer available in their small villages. Fortunately, many churches are helping immigrants/refugees and denouncing the detention centers where the children are being held. The detention centers are located in deserts and other desolate areas where they are also referred to as the "ice boxes, hieleras, freezers, or refrigeradores" since they are so cold and ironically they're uninhabitable also! Trump knows that Lopez Obrador will do as ordered by the United States since they have secret files regarding his indiscretions. Trump said "he may be a leftist little bitch, but he is our little bitch, who will deport Central Americans!"

CHAPTER 4

L a Siguanaba was once the queen of her small village. When, her demonic spirits took over her body she would transform into a wretched ugly woman. She would take revenge and punish the alcoholics, womanizers, and wife beaters. But she kept that demonic side of herself a top secret. Some say that she took on the appearance of a horse's face at night. She would roam the villages of not just El Salvador, but also Guatemala, Honduras, Costa Rica, Dominican Republica, Nicaragua, and even Southern Mexico. She is known as Cigua in Honduras, Cegua in Costa Rica, and Ciguapa in the Dominican Republic. During the day, she would evolve to remain an exotic, older, beautifully kept older lady. When she was enraged, she would take on the diabolic/demonic appearance. She purposely did not grow older and remained beautiful when she wanted to. With her wicked, evil appearance she would make men go crazy. She would wail with laughter or cries to the point that men would go mad. Some would become blind, deaf, or simply crazy. She would take their souls. They would walk around the villages, small towns, and cities muttering nonsense and sharing their horrific experiences with La Siguanaba. They would share how she would be washing clothes or underwear in the streams and how she would seduce them with her natural beauty. Once they would get all hot and bothered with her she would reveal her true identity. She looked and sounded horrific. She would hypnotize and put a spell on the men to go crazy. Los jugaba y los dejaba todos dundos, babosos, o locos. Quedaban todos bobos. This was sweet revenge for her. If she pleased, she would simply choke them to death. She took sexual pleasure when she would choke the shit out of them. Literally. Some men erroneously thought that they were engaging in sado*masochism* — yes — for the first minute or two. Then, it was plain torture — a lo erótico vía La Siguanaba. She was sadistica.

In the United States, she had evolved to become a billionaire. An empty billionaire. She had lost her way along the way — just like her favorite singer Boy George; he was a famous 1980s singer with Culture Club who descended into drug/alcohol addictions but eventually began to recover. She loved how he was proud of being gay and extravagant. She also greatly admired Freddie Mercury and David Bowie for being flamboyant and for believing in their God given, artistic and musical talents. She loved playing the songs of *Heroes* by David Bowie and *Don't Stop Me Now* by Freddie Mercury.

When she would become despondent and lonely, she would listen to Boy George's song *Time* and she would wear all white, while drinking red wine. She sometimes would even dress up as Boy George.

The wine would take her back to those memories. Those terrible memories. Once she had a third glass of red wine, she would begin listening to Rocio Durcal's "Como han pasado los años" and to Julio Iglesias. She was a romantic by nature.

She began to remember how El Cadejo had seduced her and tricked her. The motherfucker was the leader of a human smuggling ring — trata de mujeres — el hijo de la gran puta.

The motherfucker was raised in a *casa de putas* — and his mom was the *mera* of the prostitution ring. He learned to disrespect women — he had no human decency. He merely saw women as sex objects. He began having sexual experiences as a child since he was used as a toy by the *burdeleras*. Las putas del burdel would call him mi niño lindo y el Cipotillo vergudo. They would play Camilo Sesto, Julio Iglesias, Jose Jose,

Roberto Carlos love songs while they taught El Cadejo how to screw. He was la máquina sexual. When he would misbehave, le daban unas pijiadas and he was forced to lick salt off their backs and butts. They dehumanized him, just how the pimps and sex traffickers had dehumanized them. They became the oppressors. La Siguanaba was lured into his web of lies and pimp tricks. He seduced her and even married her. He impregnated her with semi evil twins: El Cipitio and El Duende. Making La Siguanaba go mad to the point of drowning one of her offspring: El Cipitio. She chose not to drown El Duende since she chose to hide him in her ample bosom. She did not like the fact that El Cipitio was dark skin, had a pot belly, and he was born with his feet backwards. She was undiagnosed with postpartum depression. She was simply labeled *la loca.* People would blast "y los chicos del barrio le llamaban loca" — a pop song that was very popular in 1990s.

Her rage would make her convert from a beautiful, voluptuous, woman to a wicked, disgusting looking demon — with long, nasty hair, tits dragging on the ground, and sharp pointy nails, that served a razor blades. She would slash unfaithful men that would wander the country roads late at night. She would howl and cry, cry to the top of her lungs. To the point of making men go fucking crazy. She would sometimes wear or carry a golden comb, un peine de oro. She particularly liked cutting off the dicks of abusive men with her razor blade fingernails. She would then bake the penises and made them into morongas that she would sale at a Mercado and local mesones. People loved them, especially the ones that were thick, juicy, and full of blood. They thought that they were eating pig meat, but they were eating human dick meat. She howled in laughter when other dumb ass men would eat the morongas while La Chanchona music played in the background. The drunkards loved listening to Los Temerarios while eating moronga. Dumb

17

asses would keep ordering more Pilsener, Regias, and Golden beers to make the blood tastier with beer alcohol. Once they would devour the morongas, they would order cocteles de conchas. Fully borrachos, they would scream "que viva La Selecta." Even though they rarely win any futbol games.

El Cadejo had unleashed the worse in her. He was truly a low life pimp. He had seduced thousands of campesina young girls, luring them with romantic trickery. He would whisper in their ears "que hermosa eres — como una flor de primavera." He loved to sweet talk. They would fall for his shitty charm and amateur poetry. He recruited and promised them jobs, and to become models. He would take them to Guatemala, Honduras, Belize, Nicaragua, Mexico, and even to the United States. He would sell them to the cartels and human traffickers for $5,000 each. He would label their bodies with his evil tattoo imprint: EL CADEJO — with a paw of a wolf, as his trademark. That piece of shit treated women like as if they were cattle. He was also proud of his tattooed prison number A4242. It was a badge of honor and he would often show it off to women.

La Siguanaba would eventually teach him a lesson. She would show everyone that she could become the first female Pope in the Vatican. She would have to make a deal with the devil himself, El Cadejo who had taken on the persona of El Zek. Her plan was to ultimately unlock the mystery in how to fully destroy El Cadejo. The Pope in the Vatican was the only one who had the secret formula/exorcism ritual to destroy the evil El Cadejo. This was her ultimate ulterior motive — to obtain the secret formula to fully take away the supernatural, satanic powers of El Cadejo. She was Machiavellian at heart and would ultimately *use* El Cadejo to get what she wanted and then she would dispose of him. Como una bolsa de basura. She would often refer to El Cadejo as *trash.*

However, for her own selfish self-interest, she needed the most evil fucking political consultant and El Cadejo, also known as El Zek. could deliver support from the Catholic Church. Once La Siguanaba had become The Pope, then she would no longer need him anymore. Her ultimate plan was to murder him. She loved the phrase that stated, "revenge is a dish best served cold." She knew that sooner or later El Cadejo would turn on her and would try to murder her. His demonic, evil, spirit was stronger than any good intentions. She had no choice but to murder his ass.

CHAPTER 5

Eventually, El Zek was deported from Russia and roamed through many other countries before he ended up establishing a new town called Armenia en Sonsonate, El Salvador. He had an ingenious business plan in mind. He produced and sold fake Salvadoran citizenship passports to over 20,000 Russian and Middle Eastern Armenians so that they could move to El Salvador. They blended in perfectly with the Guanaco culture and even embraced the term "Turcos" even though most were not Turks — they were of Middle Eastern descent. They learned to make pupusas and established clothing, salt processing, maquilas, car and motorcycle dealerships.

They became instant millionaires since the Guanacos were great workers who could easily be exploited since the Spanish had colonized them and had taught them to accept oppression and exploitation by foreigners. They taught them to love anything foreign and to denigrate and exploit their own people to please the foreigners. Similar to Filipino's colonization process. Filipino's were taught to love their oppressors to be forever grateful for obtaining a job from the exploiter.

They even learned to admire and love President Duterte even though he had ordered the murder of their drug addicted sons and daughters. They began to internalize violence as a method of resolution. Similar to how Salvadorans also learned and internalized violence as an everyday occurrence. Beating of their sons and daughters was perceived as normal — but there is nothing normal about beatings, torture, and constant insults.

Some children began to believe that their name was truly "hijo de la gran puta, maldito, culero, bastardo, y pendejo." Sometimes the children would feel a sense of emptiness if their mother or father had not called them one of these degrading words. They thought it was love. After the beatings, the perpetrators would tell the children "si se portan bien, no les pegaré con la cuerda electrica y el lazo mojado." They were acting just like the slave owners who loved torturing. La Siguanaba would tell her comadres and compadres, "If you want to see what slavery is truly about — check out the movie *Twelve Years a Slave*. That shit is for reals." The original names, languages, and traditions were taken away from the human beings that were forcefully kidnapped from Africa as a Bob Marley says in his song Buffalo Soldier.

Buffalo Soldier, dreadlock Rasta
There was a Buffalo Soldier
In the heart of America
Stolen from Africa, brought to America
Fighting on arrival, fighting for survival...
If you know your history
Then you would know where you coming from
Then you wouldn't have to ask me
Who the heck do I think I am?

La Siguanaba told El Cadejo "To this day, the lands and properties of the black communities throughout the United States, continue to be stolen through fraud. Reparations for the descendants of slaves is a real issue that must be addressed and remedied. When I become Pope, we will return the stolen lands!"

In El Salvador, many of the mestiza Guanaca daughter's dream was to marry a foreigner — to obtain a foreign sounding last name. The colonizers also taught *the colonized* envy and jealousy as an everyday occurrence. They could not stand another guanaco succeeding or doing good. If some guanacos did not accept the 'envy or jealousy' mentality, if they resisted, they were tortured and murdered. El Zek knew that the strategy of *divide and conquer* would usually work to keep colonized people in their place. Unfortunately, some fuckers had it in their genetics to be jealous and envious by nature. They were the most dangerous and cruel fuckers that hate their own people. These evil fuckers don't even have to be paid to harm people. They enjoy it and offer their evil services on a pro bono basis. El Zek was *el cholero* of the oppressors.

El Zek's ultimate goal was to prepare, finance, and run Turcos to become presidente of El Salvador. The Spaniards and British developed a psychological manual to be implemented with the colonized. They would even hire African slaves to become the overseers and controllers of the colonized lands. If the indigenous resisted, the black slave oversees would beat the shit of them. Eventually, blacks and indigenous began to mix, since millions of black slaves were brought to work the lands in Atlantic sea coastal towns throughout Latin America. They landed in the eastern side of Mexico, Belize, Honduras, Nicaragua, Costa Rica, Panama, Brazil, and many other countries. Of course, these countries denied having African roots, even to this day! The denial is tremendous and La Siguanaba would say to herself "estos cerotes que se creen europeos con el pelo todo colocho. Indios babosos!"

El Zek (El Cadejo) even took over the water distribution system in El Salvador and became the owner of reservoirs and wells. With the unlimited power of water ownership — he established a beer company called El Zek beer and he also created Tic Tac as a diluted vodka drink. He wanted natives to become addicted alcoholics. To be easily controlled and for the masses to be sedated. They would become more docile and would be taught to hate their own people, trained to commit untold tortures and murders. To the point where the mestizos would become haters of their own people. El Cadejo took ownership of rivers and wells so that he could have limitless access to water to be converted into billions of beers that would be sold to the dundo borrachos. He also implemented small businesses where conchas and beer were sold to the masses. It was his ingenious plan to slowly make the population addicted to Tic Tac and El Zek beers.

El Zek also secured all of the contracts with the *Coca Cola* company. He pretty much took the lakes, reservoirs, and drinking water sources — to be diverted and given unlimited access to make *Coca Cola*. A lot of the villages were left with no drinking water and many of the indigenous had to walk miles and miles to get drinking water from remote locations. If they crossed the *Coca Cola* company property lines they were shot to death. El Zek even considered replacing the Salvadoran flag symbol with the Coca Cola trademark image. He would try to convince the FMLN leadership that red and white Coca Cola colors match the FMLN colors and that it would be a perfect. El Zek even thought of offering to double the campaign contributions that Brazil and Venezuela made to the Mauricio Funes presidential campaign. He knew that democracy and all individuals have a price to be bought off. Funesto was greedy and adored money. In order to avoid prosecution, he ran to Nicaragua and was given Nicaraguan citizenship by Daniel Ortega, president of Nicaragua.

El Zek knew that he had to infiltrate the leftist political party of El Salvador, the Farabundo Marti para la Liberacion Nacional – FMLN in order to make his devious plans a reality. He ran candidates on populist platforms, and he stole the ideas of other legendary revolutionaries. He plagiarized the ideas and speeches of Simon Bolivar, Napoleon, and Nelson Mandela. El Zek biggest personal secret and ambition was to become presidente de El Salvador. He wanted to also change the Salvadoran constitution so that he could be president of El Salvador for life. He wanted to emulate Fidel Castro, Hugo Chavez, Daniel Ortega, and Nicolas Maduro from Venezuela. He wanted private chefs and strippers to be at his disposal at all times. He wanted a statue made out of gold to be made in his image. One of his other secrets was to get rid of the Salvadoran monetary system called *colones* — to be replaced by the dollar monetary system. His ultimate goal was to conduct money laundering with dollars and through the corrupt Salvadoran banking system. He would serve as the middleman for the Russian oligarchs to launder money any way they pleased. He just needed established political parties to do so and the FMLN and Arena (the National Republican Alliance) were perfect. He recruited and ran Francisco Flores and Tony Saca for Arena. Then, he recruited the FMLN's chosen man, Mauricio Funes to run for the presidency. He knew "que les valía verga el pueblo." While the population was the being extorted, tortured, and murdered by the criminals, the party leaders were enjoying conchas, langostas, y cervezas at the beach and taking government paid trips to Disney World in Florida and going on wild spending sprees in Beverly Hills. They also loved making banking deals with Panama and Costa Rica. Panama was a perfect haven for illegal banking transactions.

He loved how some so-called leftist leaders embraced Socialism/Communism to fit their own personal political interest and self-enriching rackets. Just like the good old Capitalists. El Cadejo and his political candidates loved to eat the best cattle steaks with big *Coca Colas* and *Corona* beer, while watching their favorite Disney movies such as *Dumbo and Mary Poppins.*

Socialism and Capitalism had one common denominator: human greed for money and power.

CHAPTER 6

Now getting back to La Siguanaba.

The big fucking dilemma for La Siguanaba was how to become a member of a respected church in Los Angeles to be able to gain the trust of the congregation and priest. Her goal was to take online religious courses in order to become eligible to become the first female Catholic priest. She was ingenious — she would do the online Priest Preparation Program. Similar to the required Teacher Credential Programs that require individuals to take university courses and to pass tons of Pearson's test in order to become a credentialed teacher. This is a billion-dollar profiteering racket. Anyone can hire someone else to take the online courses and tests. Many teachers, nurses, police officers, paramedics, fire fighters know that they can take state and federal required test online, and all they have to do is pay someone to take these test/course for them online and submit them.

To cover her online Priest Preparation Program and to appear more legit, she decided to join Holy Ghost Church in San Gabriel, CA. She felt that she could blend very well with the Latino, Asian, and Anglo communities. She loved to sing the himnos. She also joined All Angels and Sinners Church in Pasadena to join alliances with the progressive community.

She became buddies with Holy Ghost Church's priest, el Padre Santo (Priest Sainthood), and asked him if she could shadow him. She wanted to learn all the tricks of being a devout priest. The only part that she did not like was how the priest would whip himself every time he looked at her ass. He would secretly play "Do you remember" by Earth, Wind, and Fire while he would fantasize screwing La Siguanaba while he jerked off to her photos. He had done a deep, background check on her and found old photographs of her posing for Smooth magazine and Low Rider magazines.

She had to wear loose clothing to avoid all of the fuzz when she would attend church. All of the men would stop listening to the priest since they would literally become hypnotized with her big gluteus maximus — jello, wobbling nalgas. Men would kneel so long, since they had a hard on, and stare so much that they would say to each other "se me durmieron los huevos — pero los pinches ojos no. El pinche problema es que se me quedó dura la pinga." And his friend did a rebuttal "fool, you ain't no Cubano — why you saying pinga? Este guey quiere ser Pit Bull."

La Siguanaba didn't give a fuck. She took the online classes and obtained A's in all of them since Priest Sainthood would provide free tutoring services to her late at night — with only candlelight. He figured that he would avoid seeing her ass with candlelight in the church basement. He attended and graduated from priest preparatory school/universities in Italy/El Vaticano. His best friend was none other than Pope Chastity — they were classmates in The Vatican priest university. They both loved chamomile tea while reading the bible. They loved reciting and humming to monk songs. They still corresponded via email and sometimes would even send erotic pictures to each other. One day, Padre Santo could not resist, and he sent explicit photos of La Siguanaba to Pope Chastity. Pope Chastity said "Santo Dios! Esto es un pecado — no puedo resistir la sensacion sexual" — and he came on himself while viewing the Smooth magazine photos.

The only person that found out the Priest Sainthood's secret, close friendship with Pope Chastity was La Siguanaba. She promised and swore on the bible that she would never divulge their little secret. Priest Sainthood was so happy and told her that she reminded him of Joan of Arc since he had written his PhD thesis based on Joan of Arc. What a compliment! They became so chummy that the priest began to tell La Siguanaba — "don't bitch out on me girl." Which pretty much meant that she would not quit the process to become the first female priest of the worldwide Catholic church. A lot was riding on her. She had to prove that she was a chingona and that she would not quit. Priest Sainthood even bought a gift for La Siguanaba, DIANA'S brand of semillas de marañón, cashew seeds, since he knew she loved authentic cashew seeds since it reminded her of her childhood when cashew seeds were burned over fire — to be roasted and eaten. She loved to see the chispitas from the seeds when roasted. Once she tasted the cashew seeds from DIANA'S corporation, she flipped. She told Father Sainthood, "estas mierdas saben a cacahuates con leche y manteca. Estas cochinadas no son originales y tienen sabor a PLANTERS peanuts." Father Sainthood apologized and begged for forgiveness. La Siguanaba responded by saying "está bien cipote cagado. Esas chingaderas no son originales."

She learned about St. Francis of Assisi, St. Tomas Aquinas, and about the rumors that a female Pope had existed in the past but that the church had covered it up and acted as if it was a fantasy, made up story. She asked Pope Sainthood about it — and he took her through the tunnels underneath Pasadena. They ended up at the NASA top secret, national security area located in La Canada Flintridge – little Area 51. He led her to the Catholic Church secret vault. He again made her swear that she would never ever divulge the location and content secrets. He opened the centuries old files that documented Pope Joan's true existence from 855 AD to 857 AD. She was first transgender female Pope during the Middle Ages. She began her career as a monk but eventually became the private assistant to the Pope in

854 AD. She eventually became the lover of the Pope Benedict III. His nickname was VeniDick among the British clergy. Monk Joan was born a natural genius. She could read anything in literature and understand its true meaning, she wrote her own books and poetry. She did not have to co-write/collaborate shit cause' she was talented. She knew that motherfuckers would try to plagiarize and steal her creative ideas. She knew that motherfuckers would try to disrespect her copyrights and trademarks that she had already submitted and certified with the Vatican Church. She knew math and science at all levels — she could relate to the rich and poor. She did not have to collaborate with assholes that would steal her original ideas. She learned her lesson the hard way once, a duo of theater performers wanted to do a play regarding her life and she had written the script already and they deceitfully asked her to send the word file via messenger pigeons. Microsoft Word did not exist in the 9th Century. They simply wanted to plagiarize her work and claim it as their own. The theater performers said that Monk Joan was selfish. She said to them "I am no pendeja, cerote brothers."

Monk Joan was so popular and effective — she eventually rose to become a bishop in the Vatican. Eventually, she was promoted to become Pope Joan since she poisoned Pope Benedict because he kept screwing all of the nuns. Monk Joan said, "my life peaked when I was three years old — after than it was all downhill." Her prophetic words are embedded on the Vatican church wall.

La Siguanaba would simply copy the strategy created by Pope Joan. She would dress as Boy George to become the Pope! She loved shopping at Costco, Marshall's, and Ross since they had the best discounts and similar clothing that Boy George wore. Once in a while she would shop at Target but avoided being seen there since it was a French owned company. She wanted to project an image that she supported Made in America and Italian products — since the Vatican is located in Italy.

She wanted to look just like Boy George, so she would also go to American Apparel to get 80's neon style clothing. What an ingenious plan. She thought of creating a theme or motto to confirm her masculinity and she came up with 'suck my balls.' But she figured it may not resonate with law abiding, Christian/ Catholic conservatives.

La Siguanaba decided to hire El Cadejo as her political consultant so that he could come up with catchy phrases that would resonate with the masses. He had gained tremendous experience since he formerly worked at Hallmark gift cards. He was the chief consultant in coming up with lovely, heart-warming phrases. That fucker was influenced through Air Supply music. He would play Air Supply's best hits through YouTube. He loved blasting *Lost In Love* and *Making Love Out Of Nothing At All*. He loved that lead singer Russell Hitchcock had colocho hair – puro Salvi.

CHAPTER 7

They met at a Starbucks to discuss her campaign to become the first female Catholic Pope. She ordered a venti *Frappuccino* since she wanted to feel Italiana that day. She told El Cadejo that they would put their differences aside for the campaign and that she would pay him $1 million in cash. Pure $100 bills that still had the distinct smell from the U.S. Treasury Department print shop.

Sitting at the Starbucks took her back to her small village in El Salvador where as a child she had to work the coffee fields. She would pick cotton and coffee. She remembered how the landowners cheated and tricked the *campesinos* with rigged weigh scales. They would say — "it's only 50 *lbs*" when in fact it was 100 *lbs*. They would get paid 5 *colones* for the whole day. They would not even dare to look at the face of the capataz, el big jefe *vendido* — since they were afraid that they would get fired.

They were taught to keep their heads down, to not make direct eye contact, and to just answer as "si señor, lo que Ud. diga." Once they started watching Cantinflas movies they started to adopt certain Mexicans terms such as "mande." Which pretty much means whatever you command.

While sitting there, La Siguanaba could smell the coffee brewing and she wondered if the coffee was from Guatemala or El Salvador. Coffee picked by children who helped their mothers and fathers so that they can put food on the table: tortillas con sal, maybe some frijoles bejucos, and if it is a good day — they may have some queso duro.

But she snapped out of her daydreaming and came back to reality in the U.S.A. the land of milk and honey. When she did not get her coffee on time, she went into a rage and told the barrista, "do you know who I am? I am a fucking billionaire and wealthier than your fucking boss Howard Schultz — fuck you and fuck him! — give me my motherfucker café now you little bitch."

El Cadejo was dumbfounded and he told her that she needed to clean up her appearance to be perceived more of a monja/nun. She could no longer wear Prada, Gucci, Valentino, and other expensive shit. That was his first campaign demand.

He also recommended that she start tipping Starbucks barristas to build goodwill. She decided to tip $1 to the Starbuck barrista. As she dumped the dollar in the tips jar near the cashier — she said, "this is for your great customer service and future higher education." The barista was speechless. First, La Siguanaba was a bitch and then she was further offensive and condescending. The barista was livid, and she took out her fury on the next customer who asked to use the restroom. It just happened to be a black man. The white barista told him "fuck you man, you have to fucking buy a cup of coffee before I let you use *my* restroom."

The customer put on his Malcolm X cap and busted out with his NAACP membership card. His rebuttal was eloquent "Dear lady, I have read every Frederick Douglas biography, I listen to Fela Kuti on my streaming Apple iTunes, and let me inform you: I will sue your ass!" Next thing you knew, Al Sharpton was outside protesting with a sign that read "Fuck Starbucks, bitches be racist." Howard Schultz personally met with Al Sharpton and the NAACP member, he gave him a personal $1 million check to Al and an additional $1 million to the disgruntled customer. All of a sudden, Howard announced that he would have a *Kumbaya, My Lord* racial justice training day. Staff members were required to stand in a circle and hold hands while they described their struggles with wearing a green apron, all day. Tears flowed freely. Al Sharpton told Jesse Jackson, "that dumb motherfucker gave me a $1 million check — why don't you hit him up too?" Jesse Jackson responded by saying, "Praise the Lord, we will pass out the plato de ofrendas — I learned that from my Latino Pastor friend from La Luz del Mundo who lives like a king and has many queens on the side." They both laughed to the bank.

El Cadejo loved La Siguanaba's folksy vocabulary but also asked her to tone it down since she would be seeking the highest position within the Catholic Church: El Papa or better yet La Papa, La Papisa. La Siguanaba burst into laughter just like Selena would do and said "La Papisa que te pisa."

First, she would need to appear to be male. So, El Cadejo recommended that she continue to adopt the Boy George look to appear gender neutral and to confuse the congregations. If they would bring up the issue of her gender — El Cadejo advised her to begin screaming that it was gender discrimination/sexual harassment and to never ask her that question again. Sometimes she would ask a rhetorical question — "was Freddie Mercury ever asked whether he was gay? Hell no. So, don't ask me discriminatory questions." She even quoted Juan Gabriel at time and she would paraphrase his statement "lo que se ve, no se pregunta."

El Cadejo offered to bring the band *Intocable* to play at Holy Ghost Church and to play at the Los Angeles Coliseum. He specifically requested for *Intocable* to play "Tu Eres Mi Droga" and to be dedicated to La Siguanaba. The keynote speaker would be none other than La Siguanaba — sponsored by Hershey's company and *Coca-Cola*. One bar of free chocolate, for each attendee, and one can of *Coca-Cola* to be distributed to the masses. Who would officiate the mass? None other than Pope Chastity — all the way from El Vaticano. However, El Papa was required to do an FBI and Department of Justice fingerprint background check in order to receive a visa to enter the United States. President Donald Trump was not fucking around. Trump was so thrilled to find out that Pope Chastity had received and viewed explicit photos of La Siguanaba. Trump told his closest technology spies "this is magnificent. The Pope is now in my back pocket. I will blackmail his ass." What Trump did not realize, was that La Siguanaba had him in her back pocket since she had recorded their screwing session in Epstein's little sex island mansion. She also recorded his private phone conversations with the president of Ukraine. La Siguanaba was keeping her relationship with Melania Trump the ultimate secret. The ace card.

During their romantic pillow talk, La Siguanaba confided in Melania one of her past live's secrets: she was a noblewoman from Okunevo, Siberia. Thousands of years before she had lived in Siberia and she was the queen of her ancient Okunev culture. The Okunev were spreadout throughout Siberia and even migrated to parts of Kazakhstan. The Okunev culture can be traced to present day Republic of Khakassia. The Okunev migrated through the Alaskan Bering Strait and walked south to present day Canada, United States, Mexico, and Central America. Rumor circulated in Okunevo, Siberia that the 'noblewoman' had drowned her son and then committed suicide. They were buried but the spirit of La Siguanaba and El Cipitio came back to live and that they migrated to present day America. Rumor also circulated that she kept the *chelito* (El Duende) son alive under her big breasts. The villagers in Okunevo recounted a story that a lady in a white gown would roam the local lake – crying and howling. Looking for her children. After hearing such a fantastic story Melania told La Siguanaba "we are blood sisters, long live Siberia, Slovenia, and El Salvador! I will support you in your quest to become the first female Pope. I give to you a gift of a lucky *crystal* that came from a meteorite that landed in a lake in Slovania. It has supernatural powers and it will protect you from all evil." La Siguanaba hugged Melania and they both cried together. Their bond was sealed por vida.

La Siguanaba was so nervous since she had to be the keynote speaker in front of over 100,000 people! But now she carried the magic crystal that gave her additional supernatural powers and confidence. La Siguanaba decided to borrow a popular line from pop culture. She would title her speech "Wakanda Forever." She wanted to portray herself as a female Mayan hero — that the Catholic Church had colonized her people but that her roots and resiliency mattered. She was La Princesa Maya who also had Afro roots. She would tell her friend "ain't no shame in being thick, girl."

She was nervous that her blouse and tight ass skirt had lint. She ordered a dozen lint cleaning rollers. She did not want to appear messy. She wanted to look exquisite for the occasion. She asked her assistant to role the lint cleaner dozens of times to take away any threads from her clothing. The assistant left one small piece of lint and La Siguanaba went ghetto on him. She told him "te voy a meter mis tacones en tu culo." The assistant was somewhat insulted but he sorta like the idea since he was used to big dildos and getting methamphetamine pills shuffed up his ass. The pills stimulated his creativity and sexual drive. He also liked to sprinkle cocaine powder on penises, then he would sniff the cocaine before he would perform head. La Siguanaba loved firing people to feel a sense of power and superiority. She called in her assistant and told him "this is not working for me, bye bitch."

La Siguanaba religiously viewed Hitler speech videos, and she would also observe Martin Luther King, Jr. and Malcolm speeches. She chose to emulate and combine their oratorical skills. During her Google Scholar research, La Siguanaba was shocked to find out that Hitler's original last name was Solomon and that he had Jewish roots! The crazy fuck, Adolf Hitler, had ordered the murder of his Jewish family and destruction of his Jewish roots through the annihilation of his hometown. A complete cover up took place by the Third Reich/Nazi party. Hitler detested his abusive father, who had Jewish blood. Hitler had an extremely questionable close relationship with his mother that created great friction with his father. La Siguanaba cracked up and said "este hijo de la gran puta si que estaba loco! Esta mierda del Oedipus complex es la neta!"

La Siguanaba chose to give her speech at the Los Angeles Coliseum since it had so much history and meaning to her since she used to spend a lot of time at the Museum of Natural History and even went to see Los Bukis and Los Temerarios at the L.A. Sports Arena. She loved the darkness and coolness of the museum. One time she even hid in the restroom and spent the night at the museum. She wanted to sleep next to the polar bears section. She loved being able to walk around to see the dinosaur displays and precious stones section. She decided that she would write her speech at the museum since it inspired her creativity, imagination. She took a few joints of weed to further motivate her thoughts and dreams. She told the animal displays "lets burn this motherfucker joints to get true inspiration."

She titled her speech *Wukanga Forever,* her speech would include a message of the history of slavery, of tolerance and inclusion of immigrants, a message of inspiration for all. She would play *America* by Neil Diamond in the background and images of historical slave photos, the struggles and sacrifices of immigrants, and a message of unity. She also explained how the spirits of our ancestors fly in the air. How they souls roam the earth. Especially the immigrants and slaves that have been murdered. Their spirits are forever in turmoil.

She wanted to bring back their spirits/souls through her speech.

El Cadejo decided to take on the nickname of the Brown Puma — to play on the Black Panther hero theme. He said "I am the Brown Mayan Puma" who will help to get La Siguanaba to become the first female Pope. He also decided to give La Siguanaba a catchy nickname, The Mayan Queen — La Reina Maya. La Siguanaba se hecho una carcajada and said "me encanta esa mierda. ¡Yo soy La Reina Maya, hijos de la gran puta!"

El Cadejo created an Instagram account with the hashtag that said #TheMayanQueen. In just one day she received over 100 million followers. Then, she decided to drop $2 million dollars to recruit followers/likes from throughout the world. In one week, she obtained over 1 billion followers. El Cadejo knew secret algorithms and he targeted Catholic church members. Before La Siguanaba knew it, she had over 2 billion faithful followers. She had an extraordinary level of support, a loyal base. Many people had told El Cadejo that it is all about exposure, and he eventually decided to start replying "fuck that stupid shit, exposure my ass! Imagine if I would expose my dick in the Mojave Desert — it would burn off, bitches!" He had become a fucking genius with social media. He knew that he would have to come up with outrageous comments and videos featuring La Siguanaba. El Cadejo was so resourceful that he was able to get Anastasia Kvitko to not just follow La Siguanaba on Twitter and Instagram — but to actually endorse her efforts to become the first female Pope. El Cadejo flew La Siguanaba to Russia and a photo shoot was done with Anastasia Kvitko and La Siguanaba. Anastasia's followers went bananas and fully embraced and supported La Siguanaba. Billions of Google searches were traced via the Google search engine that found that the most asked question of the week was "whose ass is bigger La Siguanaba or Anastasia Kvitko?

El Cadejo decided to do thirty-second to one-minute short video clips featuring the life and struggles of La Siguanaba. He came up with the idea to include Sandy Caldera's Christian music in the background. He bought a Go Pro camera to capture the essence of La Siguanaba while she spoke through her heart and soul.

The first one-minute video featured La Siguanaba's humble beginnings that made sure to hide the negatives of her past. No one, no one could find out that she had drowned her twin sons — well, actually, one. She drowned El Cipitio since he was born with dark skin, a big belly, and feet backward. She decided to keep El Duende alive by hiding him under her huge tits. However, she eventually had to give him up for adoption.

The guilt of her wicked act haunted her throughout her life. She would walk around the rural areas of El Salvador at night wailing and crying. Asking to herself "donde estan mis hijos?" She would take on a diabolic, evil look. Her skin would become deadly pale, with sagging bags under her eyes, and razor-sharp long nails. Her voluptuous butt would sink and sag. Her hair would grow extremely long and she would wear a see-through white gown where you could see her horrific sagging breast, reaching the ground. Her nipples were shriveled like raisins. Her eyes were blood red. Her shrieks would make men go crazy when they would see her and hear her high shriek cries.

Initially, she would seduce them through her amazing Mayan beauty. Once they would get close to her, she would hypnotize them with her blood, red eyes. If she wanted to — she would fuck them and the middle of them ejaculating she would become horrific. The men would go crazy and would begin to blab and walk around saying incoherent things. She would throw carcajadas — great laughs that would make the men become semi deaf. She was taking revenge since she perceived these men as mujeriegos. She left the men "jugados." She fucking hated womanizers/players. They reminded her of El Cadejo. The evil Cadejo — El Cadejo negro.

However, now the kind Cadejo — El Cadejo blanco - was running her campaign and she had partially forgiven him, for now. She was so glad that the fucker had decided to become benevolent. They both had to repress their evil sides. They represent humanity and the eternal struggle of good vs. evil. Most humans struggle since each has a good and evil side. In an enlightened moment El Cadejo came up with the winning slogan: *Somos La Siguanaba. We are La Siguanaba.* At times, he took on the persona of Mike Pence to further get the support of Catholic and Christian churches. He would simply listen and nod. The congregations loved him and truly thought that they were meeting with Pence. Pence would tell the Catholic congregations that he grew watermelons and corn in his backyard. To be in touch with the proletariat, farmers, and common folk. He loved eating tamales con frijoles. Los tamales pisques y los tamales con chipilín. He would even ask for some tamales to go with extra chipilín!

El Cadejo was so ecstatic that he lit up an organic weed joint. He was beginning to develop arthritis and needed some medical weed to ease the pain. He would order his weed through Amazon Prime. Eventually the dumb fucker became addicted to fentanyl and other synthetic opioids.

He decided to begin a GoFundMe page for La Siguanaba and the top banner stated *We Are La Siguanaba.* His goal was to raise $1 billion in small donations and to get buy in from the supporters. He wanted to emulate Bernie Sanders strategy of inspiring the masses with hippie filled dreams. Of course, with a little bit of weed influenced ideas. He also did not want La Siguanaba to spend her own money on the campaign since he wanted people to invest and feel 'vested' in supporting her. Of course, the fucker Cadejo would skim some of the money to go towards his opioid addiction. He would justify it by stating that it helped him with his creativity.

He decided that La Siguanaba would be competing for the highest religious position within the Catholic Church. To become *La Papa.* No, not la pinche potato, but The Pope in female tense is La Papa, y que?

El Cadejo created an Excel spreadsheet that included a $1 billion marketing and publicity campaign budget and strategy. That fucker was ingenious. Numbers were not a big thing since he could just plug in numbers and Excel would crank out the results in a second. He learned how to use Excel through YouTube videos.

He would upload La Siguanaba thirty-second to one-minute inspirational videos onto YouTube and he would allocate tens of thousands of dollars in paid promotion/publicity to further get La Siguanaba's name out there and to incur faithful followers. He would organize Pop Ups, in an overnight manner, to raise funds for the most needy, and La Siguanaba would give out free clothes, toys, food, used boring books, to the most needy. These actions endeared her to them and began to make her a folk hero among the working class, los pobres. She even got a Pop-Up spot at the Molcajete Dominguero's and Harvest Arts & Crafts Festivals to sale merchandise (t-shirts, purses, and pins) that promoted her image next to Frida Kahlo and Mother Teresa. She was a genius in self-promotion and publicity. She learned those skills from running her billion-dollar laundry service corporation. She was so resourceful that she bought a spinning wheel to make her own clothing at the pop-up vending location. People were in awe of her humility. She wanted to emulate Gandhi's tradition of using a spinning wheel to make his own clothing.

However, La Siguanaba was no Mother Teresa when it came to her sexual desires. She could not resist, and she finally hypnotized and screwed the main priest from Holy Ghost Church — Father Sainthood who eventually became known as Father Screwed. The congregation would whisper when they would call him Father Screwed, el padre cogido. She took away his virginity and innocence. She screwed him so hard that he squeeled like a little piggy while she hogged tied him. She even got him to smoke some crack and to inject some heroin. He became a love machine and a sex slave for La Siguanaba. She even forced him to pour some cocaine on her vagina and he had to lick it off. She told him "you filthy little pig, you are now my little bitch. Mi esclavo sexual" y se tiró unos pedos con carcajadas. She concluded by telling him — "now you will appoint me to be the mera Priest — la cura — que te cura el culo. You are my hoe now" That Sunday the priest stood before the congregation and cried as he said that La Siguanaba had been appointed as the new Priest — la primera cura — in all of the Catholic Church. El Priest had e-mailed the Pope in Rome and ask for his notarized signature — making La Siguanaba the first female priest ever. This was her ticket to El Vaticano.

Fuck, the headlines were outrageous. TMZ broke the news first and went live. They found and approached La Siguanaba in the parking lot of the church. Once she entered her mini Cooper the camera and reporter aggressively approached her. Harvey Levin started to interview her in Spanish since she had some indigenous features. La Siguanaba had to contain her rage. She said, "Harvey, I speak English and many other languages that I learned during Sunday school." TMZ's Harvey Levin replied, "I'm sorry Priest Siguanaba" and she accepted her apology by nodding her head and agreed to the explosive, breaking news interview.

Harvey started with a whopper. "Did you have a sexual relationship with the priest to take his place?" she answered by saying "How dare you ask me such a question? I am an honorable woman. Have you not seen my videos of me attending mass every Sunday? Why would you ask such a demonic and demeaning question to a lady?" Harvey was getting nervous since he saw some blood dripping from La Siguanaba's fingernails as she spoke. He began to panic since he could smell the sulfur and salt coming from her blood drops. Once he saw her pointy nails begin to grow razor sharp, he decided to ask his cameraman to cut the interview.

He was sweating profusely and decided to apologize. He told her off camera that he would ask soft, puffy, fluff questions and to forgive him. Harvey started over, "Ms. Siguanaba, you have made history today by becoming the first female priest ever — how do you feel on this special occasion?" La Siguanaba was gracious in her response and stated "I have sacrificed and suffered for decades to become the first female priest and I have done this to inspire young girls to believe that they can achieve anything in life. Just like Hillary Clinton, Kamala Harris, and Elizabeth Warren made us believe in our talents, I want to serve as a role model for all girls and boys, throughout the world." Harvey was mesmerized by her beauty but pretended to ignore her breasts and big ass. He blinking a lot and La Siguanaba switched into her stern teacher look and attitude and told Harvey "can you stop blinking so much."

Then, he concluded by simply saying "TMZ is making history here by interviewing the first ever female priest in the world. We wish her the very best and want to thank her profusely for agreeing to conduct the first exclusive interview. Harvey signing off from Pasadena, California.

TMZ obtained the highest ratings ever. Over 2 billion viewers throughout the world who have cable saw the interview. Young female students in Belize and Nigeria were required to write an essay regarding the life of La Siguanaba. She was becoming internationally known. She was furious that Harvey coughed during the interview. She went into a fit of rage and said "that cerote was trying to ruin my international day view. Suerte que ya tengo experiencia con entrevistas and how to deal with fucking distractions such as a pinche cough."

The cough reminded her of when she would choke men to death in El Salvador. They would gasp and cough for air. She took pleasure in murdering them, but she hated that they would spread their germs when they would cough. She was a germaphobe and did not particularly like to see or smell blood.

Therefore, she chose to choke her victims. But if she had to, she would shred them to pieces like Freddy Krueger from A Nightmare on Elm Street. The main part that she hated from her victims was their fucking cough. She would say "estos maricones no aguantan ni mierda." She would throw carcajadas while she choked their ass.

Students throughout the world were amazed that a female had become a priest. It was controversial news everywhere and the Pope had to make a formal announcement, in public, at the Vatican. He gave his speech in Spanish to make a point of tolerance and that he was fully fluent. He had received the photos of her from Priest Sainthood and he knew that La Siguanaba was fine as hell, so he wanted to personally meet her. He invited her to the Vatican — to his private VIP suite so that they could read the holy bible together.

He knew that he was sinning with his erotic thoughts. What they did not realize was that La Siguanaba was the shot caller. No man was gonna use her or control her. She was La Chingona and she would chingar/coger men, not the other way around. She read Carlos Fuentes interpretation and definition of chingar and she said "yo soy la chingona y nadie me va a chingar a mí."

She would screw the men and made them recite holy verses while they came. Some would even sing Ave Maria. She would screw the men so hard, that they would fart louder than a fucking dinosaur.

El Cadejo would crack up cause' it reminded him of when they would screw day after day. But then, the love ended, and it became a love hate relationship. El Cadejo would blast The Pretender's song "It's a Thin Line, Between Love and Hate." And he would help Crissy Hines end some parts of the song by squealing "yes, it is."

The poor motherfucker did not realize that he was about to get played by La Siguanaba.

CHAPTER 8

In the meantime, El Cadejo had to develop the final strategic plan to get La Siguanaba to become La Papa. He figured that she would have to make the leap from being the first female Priest to becoming the first female Pope.

He began to read about Steve Biko and other revolutionaries to get inspiration. He loved the following quote from Biko "The most potent weapon in the hand of the oppressor is the mind of the oppressed." He was ready to rock & roll.

He sat at La Monarca Bakery to write the campaign plan for La Siguanaba to become the first female Pope. While sitting there on Santa Monica Blvd and Western Avenue some corrupt towing company called Metro Towing Inc. decided to illegally tow his car away. It was a complete scam/fraud. He had to pay to get his car back and the wicked, evil side of El Cadejo could not be contained. He decided to boil the tow truck drivers and other corrupt employees alive and he sold the meat to King Taco — so that they could make carnitas tacos and burritos out of the corrupt fuckers. The owner and crooked attorneys are corrupt fuckers who just collect fraudulent towing fees and they love to shop at Rodeo Drive with the blood, sweat, and tears money of the working class, minority communities targeted by Metro Towing Inc. El Cadejo was infuriated to see such audacity and corruption. He hated fraudulent, lying, fuckers and referred to them as "trash." This towing company and others targeted community members in working class cities such as Hollywood, Maywood, Bell, Cudahy, Bell Gardens, Huntington Park, and

Boyle Heights since they knew that these community members were mainly immigrants who did not know how agencies enforce policies, how to file complaints, how to request fraud/corruption task force inspectors to investigate, how to request for business licenses to be shown, and many did not know how to file lawsuits to sue. When community members would call the chota/the police, the officers were trained to say, "we cannot do anything, this is a civil matter."

El Cadejo said out load, "civil matter, my ass." He reached out to the Attorney General, District Attorney, and City Attorney. He was not gonna take shit from no one and he would exercise his rights to not be oppressed. He was the modern-day Steve Biko and Fela Kuti, and he was tired of the fucking apartheid systems established in the United States. He would ask people, "have you visited the different churches in your city? Have you visited the public and charter schools? Hell no, you have not. Have you seen how segregated they are? Fuck yeah, they are segregated. Even the bible cannot unite people, so we need La Siguanaba to become that beacon of light and hope for our Catholic Church!" The audiences would roar in approval.

He was setting the groundwork for La Siguanaba to be perceived as Mother Teresa and a blend of a female Black Panther superhero.

He would end some of his speeches with Wakanda Forever and he would change the phrase to say *La Siguanaba Forever.* He decided to create Crowd Funding and Kickstarter web page links to raise $1 million to silk screen La Siguanaba's face on over 1 million t-shirts that included the phrase — La Siguanaba Forever, our Mayan Queen. These t-shirts were given out at Lakers, Dodgers, Angels, Chargers, Galaxy, and other sporting events held at the Staples Center, Coliseum, Stub Hub Center, and Union Bank Stadium.

He figured what the fuck, this would create enormous name and face recognition for La Siguanaba. His strategic campaign plan was simple. Create human-interest stories related to La Siguanaba and create empathy with her followers. His ultimate goal was to make people feel a strong connection with La Siguana to the point that they would feel that they personally knew her by her first name: La Siguanaba. El Cadejo would make La Siguanaba more famous and loved than Diego Maradona and Evita Peron, combined.

She was tired of Hollywood taking on Latin American folklore legends and making them into movies for profit. Of course, everyone would go to the movies like zombies once a 'culturally relevant' movie would be released. But she would ask El Cadejo "are any fucking schools or bookstores built from the profits of those billion dollar making movies? Hell no."

Her main interest in becoming Pope was to become owner of most of the properties and lands owned by the Catholic Church. La Siguanaba had done research through the Library of Congress and at the Los Angeles Downtown main library. She had a discovered the secrets of the Catholic Church. They were the biggest landowners in the world. That is what truly made the Catholic Church powerful and wealthy beyond belief. They also had developed a system of Baptisms — originally implemented during the colonization of Latin America, Asia, and Africa. To force parents to make their babies 'property of the church' once they were baptized. This was a system implemented to assure a constant stream of cash — in the billions — to go into the unrestricted spending accounts of high-ranking church members and priests. This was their spending money with no accountability. The fucking *diezmo* was an extortion scam implemented by the first Pope who was addicted to gambling.

He wanted force every church member to contribute 10% of their earnings to the Catholic Church. He figured, what the fuck, we will kill and beat the shit of the indigenous to get them to convert to Catholism, to get their cash to be donated to the Church. The Catholic Church became allies with the most corrupt corporations since they would both benefit through exploitation of the masses.

They figured, we need to create an alliance with the Fortune 500 CEO's to get their workers to become members of the Catholic Church. Then, the CEO's could do money laundering by donating 10% of the money they would steal from the corporations. It was a fucking true scam that was legal.

La Siguanaba thought to herself "con todo ese pinche dinero me podre comprar todo lo que me encanta — podré comprar presidentes a traves de todo el mundo!" and she would burst into laughter like The Joker. La Siguanaba was already plotting how to develop a business plan, strategic plan to launch her line of clothing titled La Siguanaba. It would be larger than Gucci, Prada, Hugo Boss, Guess, and all of the motherfucker material shit that humans crave and adore to obtain social status. "Estos pendejitos will buy my line of clothing," La Siguanaba would think to herself. She even began to daydream of launching her own perfume/cologne company that would smell of sweet nances. The main ingredient in the perfumes would include nances, zapotes, mangos, y marañones. She was ecstatic. She could not wait!

Her ulterior motives to become Pope would remain a secret. She wanted to become a bigger land developer than Rick Caruso and the Poma family from El Salvador. She wanted to have more wealth than any man in the world. She wanted to open gigantic shopping centers throughout the world. She would convert some Catholic Churches into mega, outdoor shopping centers that would include her line of clothing and perfumes. She figured that men had been taking on positions of power for self-serving purposes. Now, it was el tiempo de la mujer.

El Cadejo wanted a cut into the land-owning business/scam that La Siguanaba would implement once becoming Pope. El Cadejo had limitless greed that could not be contained. He also daydreamed of becoming a great oligarch. He wanted to surpass all of the Russian oligarchs that had used him for his genius, corrupt, political consulting services. He secretly met with the Guatemalan clown president, Jimmy Morales, to develop a strategy for Yucatan and Chiapas to be returned to Guatemala territory. The secret handshake that El Cadejo made with Jimmy was that El Cadejo would be the true owner of Yucatan and Chiapas. He wanted to be part owner of Chapin Landia. He was already imagining changing the name of Yucatan and Chiapas to Chapin Landia. El payaso Jimmy, recommended to El Cadejo to meet with president Lopez Obrador to negotiate purchasing Campeche and Tabasco.

He wanted to own castles, top of the line cars, mansions next to the beach, private jet planes, thousands of Rolex watches full of diamonds, he wanted to be coveted like Maluma. He would open his own music corporation to become the biggest record label owner. That motherfucker's greed and self-aggrandizement was limitless. He wanted to be bigger and more powerful that Putin. He would refer to Putin as "ese putito." His ulterior motive of helping La Siguanaba become The Pope, was to take a piece of the action by becoming one of the biggest landowners in the world. He had written his request on a piece of napkin while they met at Starbucks. He simply wrote *50% landowner of the Catholic Church — El Cadejo.* It was signed by La Siguanaba and him to make it an official binding contract. He threw in one tiny font line within the contract: he would have exclusive rights to sell pupusas at all of the Catholic Churches throughout the world. It stated **"El Cadejo exlusive pupusa distributor throughout the world via Catholic Church."**

The motherfucker was an evil genius. At night, he would remember his two sons — El Cipitio and El Duende. He would daydream that he had been a responsible, loving father. But he was the complete opposite. In order to forget his softy heart side, he would light up a crack pipe. He would inhale so hard that his nostrils and ass would bleed. The crack cocaine would make his brain quiver and shake a little. He loved the feeling of being high to ignore his true feelings.

Crack made him a little creative and artistic too — to the point where he would even write poetry. He handwrote a short poem to his two sons:

I miss you El Cipitio and El Duende
My heart aches
Sorry that I have been a true motherfucker dundo
One day we will bake
Together forever

In the morning, he was so embarrassed that crack made him a softy, a little pussy. His eyes were bright red when he woke up — the crack and crying all night.

He burned the poem.

El Cadejo wanted to redeem himself by helping La Siguanaba to become the first ever, official, female Pope. No matter how evil he truly was, he carried a sense of shame. He knew that he had been a deadbeat father that did not provide any financial or emotional assistance for his two sons. He knew that he had just used La Siguanaba to screw. He was a true pedazo de mierda.

No wonder La Siguanaba had various reasons to take revenge. She could not wait to be able to access the secret files within the Vatican on how to conduct exorcisms and to find the true ingredients that would eventually help to dissolve and terminate El Cadejo forever. She had to murder him before he attempted an assassination on her.

She was frustrated that El Cipitio's and El Duende's efforts were not 100% effective to truly destroy El Cadejo. She would mutter within her breath, "este hijo de la gran puta me las va a pagar, esa babosada de la sopa de pata no sirvió — voy a tener que disolver a este pendejo con algo mucho más poderoso."

La Siguanaba ultimate dream was to become an activist

Pope, to conquered equal rights for all women, for women to be respected in the labor force, to receive equal pay and equal protections. She wanted to eradicate poverty among women and children. She figured that if she became the first female Pope, her example would influence men to be more tolerant, respectful, and open to a gender-neutral society. She wanted to be bigger than Wonder Woman — she wanted to be perceived as *La Papa Super Heroica.*

But through her life sacrifices and suffering, she knew firsthand that men were inherently evil. She agreed with Hobbes the philosopher that human lives were 'short and brutish.'

Once she would be appointed La Papa, one of her first executive decisions would be to make Mary Magdalene a Saint. She knew that men had conspired to make her seem like a prostitute since she spoke her mind. One of the key weapons to silence a social justice activist was to simply discredit them and to create vicious rumors and lies, to destroy the integrity of the person. The corrupt leaders of the Church had succeeded in destroying Magdalene's reputation. Now La Siguanaba was intent into restoring her legacy as a feminist and leader who deserved to be canonized and to be made into Magdalene the Saint.

La Siguanaba asked Priest Sainthood to submit her name as a nominee to become the first female Pope. ¿Y por qué no?

The sex tapes that she had recorded of Priest Sainthood came in handy. She simply handed over a smart phone to him to view his Sadomasochism sex tapes. He almost fainted and she simply "Padre Santo usted me nominará para que yo sea la primera dama Papa, y no me mire con cara de papa, ¡viejo corrupto!" She hit it right on the nail, Padre Santo had a Mr. Potato face. Hilarious. LOL.

El Padre Santo was stressed and worried. He was so fucking annoyed with all of the paperwork that he had to read, fill out, and submit to the Vatican. The part that infuriated him the most was the fucking $500 fee charged with the application. He had to pay out of pocket but he said, "fuck that shit, I will take cash from the ofrendas to pay the fee."

He was also stressed since he had been asked to fight against environmental contamination by Industrial Areas Foundation — One L.A. organizing efforts. He drove a Hummer and a Cadillac and truly did not give a fuck about protecting the air or water. He figured, "we have enough fucking problemas with the gangsters trying to extort us." A Father from Boyle Heights asked him to join the fight in Boyle Heights against gentrification and environmental pollution. Padre Santo said that he was too busy filling out paperwork and could not join the environmental justice fight and that gentrification was God's will to improve communities. The motherfucker had taken bribes from the developers and a few local politicians who were already bought off by the polluters and billionaire developers. Some assimilated/acculturated Latinos who claimed to be from Boyle Heights, Lincoln Heights, and Highland Park were the big developers behind the construction of massive buildings and condos to get rid of the poor folks. They would drink tequila shots at the local bars and laugh since they knew that they were tricking their own people by claiming to be *activistas* but in reality they were undercover exploiters. Explotadores. Others pretended to be homeboys from the hood but in reality, they were paid *informants* to keep the police and crooked politicians informed.

Padre Santo and other activistas were also on the advisory boards of the most prominent environmental organizations that took money from the polluters. He figured that if they could care less about poor communities in South East Los Angeles, East Los Angeles, South Central Los Angeles, Long Beach/Wilmington/Harbor City areas, then so could he. "Who the fuck has really done anything to stop the polluters in the last 30 years?" We let the Exide Battery Recycling plant operate for over 30 years on a license permit and no one cared. Now

Southeast and East Los Angeles are permanently polluted. La Siguanaba would rhetorically ask "has the air and water gotten any better? Fuck no. Are working class Latinos, blacks, Asians, and whites still dying because of pollution? Fuck yeah! I rest my fucking case."

They know it's a fact that the environmental non-profit organizations are not diverse enough. So, Father Santo felt no shame in the game. He was sneaky just like the parents and accomplices in the USC student admissions scandal. They felt privileged and above the law. Luckily, a whistleblower who was busted on stock investment related corruption decided to rat on the parents and accomplices who were implementing this scam. He wanted a deal to not do jail time. The story went national/international even though these types of shenanigans had been going on for many, many decades. The sons and daughters of the elite always had access to being accepted into the top elite universities due to connections, college/university contributions from the parents, and last name recognition.

No wonder the system is rigged. Where do these students from elite universities get jobs? From the alumnus/corporations/institutions that are already connected with their parents also. Working class, minority community members have usually gotten the short end of the stick. Especially community members from Sur Centro Los Angeles. Many Latino and black kids learned to hustle by selling paletas and Frito Lay Munchies, Cheetos, with lots of Tajin and Chamoy con mucho amor. Other kids would hustle t-shirts at various sporting events just to bring some cash back to their moms or fathers to be able to buy food. Some would buy food at the Trader Joe's located in USC with food stamps. The pinche survival hustle.

La Siguanaba asked El Cadejo "who invented the hustle?" El Cadejo could not answer and La Siguanaba "pues nosotros cerote! We learned the hustle of survival from our black brothers and sisters whose land was stolen by the white folk."

She was becoming bolder now that she had bribed Padre Santo to submit the nomination to the Vatican. She ordered El Cadejo to create a hashtag title @LaSiguanabaHustle and she also requested that over 200 million shirts be printed with her face and Instagram account handle — and for 1 million shirts to be exported to each country throughout the world. She wanted to be better known that Muhammad Ali, Elvis Presley, Gandhi, Mother Teresa, and all other superheroes.

She wanted her campaign to be done a "a lo grande." She began to use ghetto words like "let's flip this bitch" which actually meant to get something done. She wanted to emulate the marketing and publicity strategy of The Avengers movie franchise. Fuck, she even wanted to be included as one of the main characters and to be the first Latina superhero. She told El Cadejo, "get me a fucking meeting with the producers/directors of Los Avengers. Pronto baboso." She was becoming emboldened and was ready to take on the world just like Freddie Mercury. She would blast *Don't Stop Me Now* to get motivated and inspired. She got on her cell phone and called Marvel Studios and said, "This is La Siguanaba, pass me through to speak to Kevin Feige." The secretary asked her, "who is La Siguanaba." The secretary was not able to pronounce the name correctly and La Siguanaba went into a fit of rage. She began to scream at the secretary and said "look bitch, I am worth billions of dollars and you do not know who I am? Pass me through Feige now or I will get your ass fired quicker than Flash." The secretary was intimidated and passed her through. La Siguanaba spoke to Feige with confidence and she lowered her voice to sound manly. She said, "Feige baby, this La Sig. Remember me?" Feige said "Not really." La Siguanaba offered to meet at Peet's Coffee and that she would pay. Feige mumbled but said "yes."

The magic, persuasive powers of La Siguanaba could get any meeting with men or women of power, especially if they ate her pupusa with loroco. She was one of them now. She was the first centroamericana ever to make it onto the Forbe's 500 list of most influential business power brokers. She would have tea meetings with Carlos Slim, Warren Buffet, and George Soros.

She wore her exquisite yellow silk skirt and blouse when she met with Feige at Peet's Coffee. She was on cloud nine. She said to Feige, "can I call you Kevin?" He was so impressed that he said "yes, please, call me Kevin." She said "o.k. Kevinito el mas chulo" He started to crack up. She busted out with a pupusa de loroco that she kept in aluminum foil in her purse. She told Kevinito to eat it with his coffee. He loved it! and shared that Leonardo DiCaprio had recommended eating pupusas. They were both now ready to get down to business. She included secret magical ingredients within the pupusa de loroco. Thus, the magical loroco.

She wanted to get down to business and said "I want to be the first Mayan female superhero, and I know that you can make it happen and you can outdo Black Panther. Why don't you have an indigenous superhero within Marvel?" Feige thought for a minute to respond, "because Latinos don't support their own." La Siguanaba se echó carcajadas.

She responded, "I am tight with The Hispanos International Media Alliance and I can get them to protest and boycott any of your upcoming movies. Are we speaking the same language now, fool?"

Feige told her "look, no one has ever spoken to me so boldly and passionately. Instead of being offended I agree with you. We do need a token female, indigenous, superhero and you can be it."

La Siguanaba took minor offense to the word 'token' but she figured what the fuck. This was her big break in Hollywood.

She could be the first ever, lead, female, Latina superhero in The Avengers. Her role would be to defend women's rights as a superhero and to promote the existence and beauty of the Mayan culture.

She decided to handwrite a brief one to page contract on the napkin of Peet's Coffee stating the following legal jargon "Marvel Comics retains the professional services of La Siguanaba, to be the main consultant for the upcoming production of The Avengers: La Siguanaba. The main character and superhero will be the first ever female, indigenous, multilingual superhero and Marvel commits to pay La Siguanaba and upfront advance/ retention fee of $1 billion to use her image and brilliant ideas. Signed by Kevin Feige and La Siguanaba."

They both signed and La Siguanaba gave a big hug to Kevinito. She told him as they said goodbye "you will not regret your little Tokenita."

Now she was certain that public opinion would be on her side. She would be in every major theater throughout the world and her superhero image would translate into helping her become the first female Pope. Her true intention was to become the biggest landowner in the world through The Catholic Church.

She could not wait to see her face on every major billboard throughout the world. She would instantly become a household name through Hollywood. She would become bigger that Roma's Yulitza.

She received a text message from Kevin, stating that they were thinking of calling the next movie: *The Avengers: La Siguanaba Lives*. She said that it sounded good and that she was expecting it to be bigger and better than Black Panther. Kevin said "for sure Sig."

La Siguanaba was becoming Americanized. She loved hot dogs, popcorn, and Coca-Cola. She wanted to break free from the stereotype that Salvi women all cook or are experts in making pupusas. But while driving, she thought of another powerful idea. She wanted pupusas to be served during worldwide screenings of *The Avengers: La Siguanaba Lives.*

She immediately called Kevin Feige and told him that

her licensing attorney would call his attorneys to amend the contract to include exclusive rights of selling pupusas at every screening of the movie and that she wanted pupusas to be prominently included in the story script. She told Feige "I want pupusas to be the secret weapon of La Siguanaba — similar to Wonder Woman's magic lazo." La Siguanaba had a soft heart at times. One of her true intentions of including pupusas to be sold at every major movie screening was for the working-class Salvi women pupusa makers to be given an opportunity to sell their pupusas at these screenings. La Siguanaba wanted these women to have a shot at making some serious cash during the showings/screenings of *The Avengers: La Siguanaba Lives.*

She figured that all these cattle ranchers, hot dog producers who were becoming billionaires through the purchasing power of the 60 million strong Latino U.S. consumers. The buyer power of Latinos is tremendous, especially the movie going crowd who is willing to spend $20 on a movie ticket, $50 on food and beverages, gasoline and parking expenses. On average two people spend $100 going to see a movie. She figured, why not help the sisters out by creating entrepreneurial opportunities with the American Capitalist system. She said, "even el Bernie Sanders knows the Capitalist hustle. He is now un multimillonario. Hasta se ve como un papasito ese viejito con todo ese billete."

CHAPTER 9

La Siguanaba at times would become philosophical. She thought of how Salvi women had been exploited for centuries and used by men. Therefore, she wanted to be the change agent. The game changer. She had the money and she just needed more power to help even the playing field. She agreed with Bernie Sanders and Elizabeth Warren, yes, the fucking system is rigged.

Why has not a woman become president of the United States? Why was Hillary Clinton vilified and demonized?

She wanted to become first female Pope to prove a point — that you did not have to have a dick to be Pope. That if we truly believed in equality — then, the Catholic Church would allow women into leadership positions. Why only men?

The most profound question that she had was — why was Mary Magdalene made out to be a prostitute by men in the church? Why was she demonized also- when in fact she was a disciple/ally of Jesus Christ? Some even say she may have been the wife of Jesus. La Siguanaba was particularly pissed off at a professor from UCLA who had intentionally described her as a 'prostitute' in a Central American anthology book. So she knew how women would also intentionally create rumors against other women, para joderlas. La Siguanaba said "where the fuck are my royalties from that anthology?"

La Siguanaba wanted to become Pope to make Mary Magdalene into a Saint. "Estos pendejos solo quieren el poder y el vino solo para ellos. Quieren seguir abusando de niños y de monjas. He dicho," concluded La Siguanaba. I will also investigate and prosecute the monjas who abuse the altar boys.

She was not fucking around. One of her first internal rules/ laws that she would establish and implement within the Catholic Church was to chop off the hands of any abusers. She was sick and tired of men taking advantage.

She knew that she had an exotic, beautiful body, but La Siguanaba wanted to be respected for her intellect. Being a superhero in *Avengers: La Siguanaba Lives* would help to shift public opinion that an indigenous, Mayan, woman could be as good or even better than Wonder Woman, Cat Woman, and the other very few women super heroes. Imagine, an indigenous woman superhero that speaks!

She knew the power of media, imagery, visuals. She knew that sexually repressed men discredited and destroyed the character and reputation of Mary Magdalene. She knew that men would try to portray her as an exotic, crazy, loca mother who had drowned her children.

But she would counter that dirty narrative with her portrayal in *Avengers: La Siguanaba Lives.*

She would be Mary Magdalene but through the character of La Siguanaba..

She figured that Marvel wanted to pretend that they were politically correct by showcasing a few minority female superhero characters. What she wanted was to be an authentic character — la mera mera de Avengers. Una mujer chingona.

She knew that in the Women's Rights Movement, it was white women leading the charge and they held all leadership positions. Minority, working class women were relegated and nonexistent in leadership and highly visible roles, similar to the Civil Rights Movement, where minority women were relegated to do the grunt work that the 'men' did not want to do themselves.

Finally, La Siguanaba felt that Avengers would do justice by having her play the leading role. She would become bigger than Wonder Woman.

She had to think of her super powers: first she would carry a pupusa de loroco to fight evil. The pupusa would be similar to Bat Man's gadgets. Her weapon of choice would be called the Pupusarang. She could throw the Pupusarang against any male attacker, and the Pupusarang would instantly chop off their dick. If necessary the Pupusarang would shoot salsa de tomato y curtido. The salsa de tomato y curtido could dissolve any motherfucker.

Her superpowers would include being immortal. She had roamed the river creeks, mountains, forests, and desolate countryside areas for centuries. She used to be stuck in El Salvador, but due to the Civil War she chose to migrate to Los United States.

She decided to embrace and to keep her beautiful look. When provoked, she would become wickedly ugly. If she was enraged and ready to kill, then would evolve to look grotesque and disgusting. She only did this at night and when she would decide to take revenge on the cheating and evil men. At night, she could transport herself to any country she pleased.

Once she set foot in the United States, she became la señora bien esculturada. She was fucking amazingly beautiful. Even the INS agents let her go and even gave her a free ride from Texas to the Washington D.C. area. One of them tried to rape her on the way there and La Siguanaba simply shredded the fool to pieces with her razor, sharp, nails. This was an additional super power. Razor sharp nails that could cut through bullet proof glass and even metal. She was not fucking around when those huge, motherfucker nails would grow. She also developed a shrieking laughter and screams that would make men go crazy or even deaf. Some would lose their minds.

She had the Pupusarang, razor sharp fingernails, shrieking, glass breaking cries, screams, and laughter, and big tits that could slap the shit out of you. And the most powerful, she was immortal. Even if someone would shoot her ass, chop her up, strangle her, she would come back to life. Now that is a scary scene, a hella ugly lady with nasty hair, razor sharp nails, big sagging tips that drag to the floor, and red shot eyes. In the ghettos of D.C, Maryland, and Virginia (the DMV), South Central, she became known as *La Chichona.* She would seduce men by asking them "quieren chiche?" She loved chilling in areas such as Sugarland in Maryland, Alexandria in Virginia, and the D.C. ghetto/barrio areas. She loved to smell the odor of pupusas. She was also proud that the number one beverage sold in Adams Morgan/Mt. Pleasant was fresco de marañon. When she visited family members in Compton, Watts, South Central Los Angeles, they would refer to her as the *The Big Titty Mama/La Chichona.* When she was in South Central Los Angeles, she would go her favorite BBQ place, Philips on Crenshaw. While she would wait for her BBQ ribs, she would literally walk across the street to visit a Christian Church. She was also trying to create bridges and alliances with various religious denominations. She figured that would only her in solidifying support internally and externally. She ultimately wanted to convert Christians, Muslims, Buddhists, and Jews to Catholics.

La Siguanaba's natural beauty was mesmerizing. She could truly hypnotize men and women via her beauty. Sometimes she could read their minds and could instinctively feel their sexual desires. Men and women would daydream and hallucinate that she would do some motorboating on them with her big tetas.

When some Anglo men from Costa Mesa, California would meet her, they would say "Me no Spanish." What they actually meant is that they do not speak Spanish. She would crack up and begin speaking with a British accent. She was hilarious. Also, Asian men assumed that she did not speak English and she would begin to speak to them in Chinese, Japanese,

Korean, Vietnamese, Cambodian languages. She had the gift of multilingualism. But she kept it low pro. She did not want to show off her natural intelligence and gift of languages. She had learned various languages by travelling to these countries through her nightly ghost/spirit teleport abilities.

El Cadejo recommended that she travel, during the day, to various countries that had millions of Catholic members. He said that he had to schedule her to visit key countries in Latin America, Europe, Africa, and Asia. He told La Siguanaba, "you have to win the hearts and minds of the people" just like Evita Peron did in Argentina.

Word finally got around that Pope Chastity would send a telegram to La Siguanaba to see if her nomination had been accepted to be considered to become Pope. Finally, the U.S. Postal Service through United Parcel Services (UPS) delivered the telegram. It had gotten lost and delivered to the wrong person in Canada. La Siguanaba said, "el Triple AAA y UPS ya no sirven como antes. Un burro podría ser más rápido."

El Cadejo and La Siguanaba were both nervous. It was a huge enveloped sealed with candle wax. Once they opened it, it was written in fucking Latin. El Cadejo said, "no mamen gueyes, ¿qué dice esta mierda?" and La Siguanaba used Google Translate from Latin to Spanish

The brief letter stated "The Vatican congratulate you for being accepted as a nominee to become Pope — your nomination will go through various committees to be further reviewed. Once a decision is made — we will blow weed smoke from the Vatican for all to smell throughout Italy and Europe, signed El Papa." La Siguanaba se hecho una carcajada and said "these fuckers cannot even spell — they forgot to include an s in the word congratulate. I should send their ass to Evans night school!"

El Cadejo knew that they had to fast track the world tour of La Siguanaba and it had to be bigger that Led Zeppelin and Queen world tours but similar in status and grandeur. El

Cadejo had to book La Siguanaba in the biggest sporting venues/ coliseums.

She would begin her tour in Mexico, Brazil, Colombia, Argentina, Guatemala, Honduras, Belize, Egypt, China, and many other countries but she planned to end her tour in Italy since the Vatican is located there. She had to develop a show that was mesmerizing visually and the content full of religious and uplifting messages. She wanted a lesson plan to be implemented that was short and sweet. She wanted the audience to have visuals, audio, and to be able to smell and taste hope in the air.

She included Enya to play music and asked Andrea Bocelli to sing Ave Maria. She asked El Cadejo to hire Steven Spielberg to develop a 5-minute video of her — sending a powerful, visually pleasing message of hope — similar to Ronald Reagan's commercials from his 1980 presidential campaign.

She wanted the smell of pupusas to be everywhere since she asked for the pupusa ladies to join her on her world tour. She wanted to introduce pupusas to every country. Her secret weapon was La Pupusarang — that also included secret food ingredients that would make people fall in love with La Siguanaba. Her secret ingredient was the Loroco plant homegrown in El Salvador. Through her travels and walks in nature, she discovered that Loroco was an aphrodisiac and that it had magical powers to instill a sense of love.

She had made thousands of men fall in love with her when they would taste and eat her Pupusa de Loroco. She would purposely place loroco in her underwear. Sometimes she would use it to cover her vagina and other times she would simply smash it on her huge butt. Men would salivate and go wild in wanting to eat her pupusa con loroco. The Pupusarang was truly powerful and she intended to provide one free pupusa de loroco to every person that would attend La Siguanaba World Tour. The loroco secret ingredient would also make women develop love and at times, sexual desires, towards La Siguanaba. The women who thought they were straight would say to each "no sé que tiene esa Siguanaba pero ese olorcito de loroco me está volviendo loquita por esas nalgotas." Sexual orientation lines would become blurry since La Siguanaba appealed to both men and women.

She decided to open the World Tour by singing the song *Time* by Culture Club. This would get the crowd going wild and happy. And of course, she would end the tour by doing a lip sync of George Michael's *Careless Whisper*. Now that song with the smell of loroco pupusas would seal the deal to obtain their support. She asked her staff to have iPad and Smart Phones ready to get each person's first, last name, address, and email. She would include every single e-mail into her Constant Contact email list that was reaching unimaginable numbers — over 1 billion email members. What better way than through e-mail for La Siguanaba to directly communicate with her followers. Also, by signing up to her email list, they were agreeing to automatically support her efforts to become the first female Pope. They also agreed to receive air dropped videos of La Siguanaba sharing her daily struggle, sacrifices, and daily achievements.

She figured that most social media were useless since people simply liked to show off and not talk about their own challenges in life. They simply wanted to be accepted, admired, and loved. La Siguanaba decided that she would become a symbol of hope and strength. Similar to Lady Gaga.

Actually, she decided to ask Lady Gaga to join her in future performances during her World Tour. La Gaga was a perfect match since she was Italian American, and they could do a duet to sing *Bad Romance*.

While she travelled to Korea, she asked BTS to join her also. Word started spreading like wildfire that La Siguanaba was the real deal. The Korean community loved her since she adored Korean BBQ beef. Public opinion was becoming massive towards her becoming the first female Pope.

Pope Chastity and his selection committee was becoming a little concerned since they never thought that La Siguanaba would manage to gain over 2 billion, committed supporters. He told el comité, "esto es algo impresionante, creo que tendremos que elegir a la primera mujer para que sea Papa. ¡Esto será algo histórico e insólito!"

Pope Chastity was shrewd and had no choice but to accept La Siguanaba as a true contender. Ultimately, the Pope was beginning to accept the fact that women are equal to men and that they should also be allowed to be priests. He ultimately also wanted Priests to be allowed to marry. He was sick and tired of the pedophile priests. He figured that they should be allowed to get married to a woman or a man. He wanted La Siguanaba to emulate U.S. laws that allow men to marry men. He was truly a closet revolutionary/radical himself.

La Siguanaba soon became a household name in most predominantly Catholic countries. The World Tour was a smash hit. Her two biggest turn outs of support were in Mexico and Italy. Two extremely pro Catholic countries. During La Siguanaba's tour in Argentina, Diego Maradona decided to do a surprise visit to express his unconditional support to La Siguanaba. He gave her a signed soccer ball and conveniently smothered his face deep into La Siguanaba's voluptuous, silky, vanilla smelling breast. And he whispered to her "me recuerda a mi madre querida."

She invited Mana, El Tri, Jaguares, and Luis Miguel to sing in the Mexican La Siguanaba World Tour. They all supported La Siguanaba and Luis Miguel developed a crush on her since La Siguanaba reminded him of his mother too. La Siguanaba would feed loroco en la boquita de Luis Miguel and would tell him "corazonsito, comaselo todo." Her breast was so comforting to Luis Miguel and to top it off she wore the same perfume de Nances that his mom would wear. The Nance perfume was a smash seller at Nordstrom and other huge retail stores. People were madly in love with the exquisite, sweet, smell. To top it off they added a yellow color to make it even more enticing and appealing to the eye. They captured the true color and essence of nances. Luis Miguel decided to dedicate *La Incondicional* song to La Siguanaba. To close the concert in el Distrito Federal (el D.F.) Luis Miguel gave a yellow rose to La Siguanaba and the crowd went bananas. He wore a yellow suit to match the banana and nance colors. Fuck, he even wore yellow underwear since he felt it would bring good luck to him and La Siguanaba.

He asked the millions of event goers to support La Siguanaba and to send Instagram and email messages to the Pope — urging him to help select La Siguanaba to become Pope. The Pope sent a message to La Siguanaba asking her to get letters of reference/recommendation from various priests and Archbishops. He told her to "keep it on the downlow — lowkey." She asked El Cadejo to develop a form/sample letter and to email it and fax it to every single Catholic Church located throughout the world. She told El Cadejo to include a prize/gift such a Pulpita de tamarindo and a free pupusa de loroco — both would be delivered through UPS or DHL delivery services. She figured that if they would eat the pupusa de loroco, they would develop a sixth sense to support her.

Once the priests/archbishops saw that they could get a free pulpita with a pupusa, they immediately signed, scanned, screen shot and sent back the letter of support. Some developing country churches only had faxes, so they faxed back the signed letters of support.

Within a day or two, El Cadejo and La Siguanaba received letters of support in the thousands.

El Cadejo told La Siguanaba, "I finished my work, I am free" and La Siguanaba responded by saying "you little bitch, you ain't done til' I say you are done. ¡Yo soy la jefa hijo de la gran puta colonizador!" He kept a poker face and while he walked away, he blasted Lady Gaga's *Poker Face* song on his portable speaker that he bought through E-Bay.

El Cadejo wanted to murder and devour her but he needed her. The fucker's self-interest overrode his rage. His self-interest for La Siguanaba was for him to have access to the gold being held in the Vatican's vaults. The total tons of gold was huge. It was the gold stolen from Latin America and sent on ship to the Vatican.

The quantity of gold was mesmerizing. Tons upon tons of gold held in underground tunnels and vaults that were a mile deep. Some of the gold was kept in original structure/form and some even had blood from the Aztecs, Mayans, and Inca indigenous slave workers.

The Catholic Church was definitely the biggest landowner in the world and also the biggest owner of gold.

El Cadejo loved to privately sing karaoke. He felt that he could have been bigger than Frank Sinatra and Elvis Presley. He loved to sing Spandau Ballet's song titled *True*. He loved how the lead singer would dress all in white. Once in a while El Cadejo would go to the local karaoke bars to sing and blend in with the crowd. He could take on the actual body and face of anyone. One night, he decided to take on the appearance of Tony Hadley. That fucker was a hit at Los Globos night club located on Sunset Blvd. People were in awe that Tony Hadley would decide to visit Los Globos.

He (El pinche Cadejo) sang *True* and he even sounded 100% like Tony Hadley. The fucker made all the women go crazy for him. He danced and romanced every single woman in the club since he had appearance of Hadley. He mesmerized many of the women and he would usually select one to take to a cheap motel to screw all night long. After screwing, he would become very hungry. He was so damn lazy that he did not want to get up to walk to McDonalds. And what would he do? He would simply decide to eat his victim. Word got around that a gentleman in a white suit would go around singing at various karaoke clubs and dance clubs throughout Los Angeles and that many women would simply disappear.

La Siguanaba read about his shenanigans in the local newspapers such as La Opinion and she would become enraged. She texted him to see her ASAP. Once he walked in, she told him "mira hijo de la gran puta, deja de andar hartándote a las cipotas de los clubs. Si seguis haciendo esas babosadas te voy a mandar a la mierda. He dicho!"

The Pope and his selection committee were truly impressed with the thousands of letters of support from various priests, nuns, and archbishops throughout the world. The Pope told the committee "esta señora sí que es popular. We will have to make a decision soon."

The committee members said we have to create another hiring committee. And the Pope told them "what the fuck, another fucking committee? Come on, twelve men already serve on the hiring committee and we need to make a decision this evening!"

He also asked if they had done a thorough background search on La Siguanaba. The committee told him that she was squeaky clean since the IRS had fully approved all of her tax returns. They only found a Driving Under the Influence (DUI) charge that was dismissed, a lawsuit against Howard Schultz since La Siguanaba claimed that her image was illegally used in the registration Trademark of Starbucks, but she lost the case, and a rumor that she had drowned her two children.

The Pope was ecstatic. He said "now we have something that we can blackmail her with. Que bien."

The Pope decided to Skype with La Siguanaba to discuss her "little problema." The Pope was calm since he had drunk one bottle of red wine from the 1400s. He loved well-kept wine. Once he was on the call, he forgot to hide the bottle and La Siguanaba was cracking up and said "ya veo que tiene buen gusto señor Papa."

The Pope cleared his throat and decided to make his voice deeper. "Look sister Siguanaba, I know about your two little children that you drowned due to your Postpartum depression. So, let's cut through the case and get to the nitty gritty."

La Siguanaba was speechless but soon regained her courage. She responded "look motherfucker, you will not blackmail me, you little bitch. Yeah, so fucking what that I drowned their ass? They cannot die anyway so shut the fuck up you pinche sinner."

The Pope became enraged and said "I can make you or break you. Just fork over $5 billion to my personal bank accounts in Switzerland and we can call it even homegirl."

La Siguanaba went pensive and felt sorry for his old ass and said "sí pues homeboy — you will get your fucking $5 billion transferred today. Just one condition — you have to sign a 'shut the fuck up' contract — are you in?" The Pope said, "sí pues, mi hija. It is a sin to judge others therefore I forgive you and absolve you Ms. Pope."

CHAPTER 10

La Siguanaba immediately sent an Instagram message to El Cadejo giving him direct orders. "Transfer $5 billion to the Pope's private bank accounts in Switzerland and Denmark. Now, you little bitch and don't ask any questions." Once the money was received The Pope was ready to make the announcement public. However, he threw in once last request. He ask La Siguanaba to get a letter of recommendation from President Donald Trump. La Siguanaba told the Pope "no hay pinche problema." She texted Trump and asked him to immediately send a letter of recommendation for her to become the next Pope or she would reveal their sex tapes to the world and his private conversations with the president of Ukraine and Russian president Putin. She told him "remember when you pissed on me after we screwed? Well I have it on tape." Trump immediately sent a PDF letter of recommendation as an attachment through Gmail. And he sent a final text stating "problem solved."

Once the Pope received the letter of recommendation from Donald Trump, he asked the twelve committee members to take a vote and it was unanimous. They all voted yes since the Pope had mentioned that he would give each one a $10 million bonus gift for their professional consultant/hiring services.

The next morning smoke began to be seen throughout the Vatican. The masses knew that a decision had been made since cannabis was being burned to signal that a decision had been reached. The smell of weed from the smoke was massive and everyone was calm and hella hungry since the smell of marijuana makes people hungry as fuck. Everyone at the Vatican and Italy were drinking coffee and eating Spumoni ice cream. Even the Italian mob was celebrating while eating pupupas de loroco and drinking fine wine.

That same morning, the sky was magnificent. Thousands of journalists/media outlets from throughout the world had descended to The Vatican.

Jorge Ramos would get the exclusive for UNIVISION and would interview La Siguanaba live — simultaneously, right after the major announcement from The Pope.

It was a majestic scene. Millions upon millions of Catholic faithful began to crowd outside of the Vatican's main cathedral. The organizing committee had done a superb job. Security was tight as hell since Donald Trump would also be attending and many heads of states did not particularly like him since he kept using the words "fabulous. fantastic, how cute, and good for you."

The other heads of states, queens and kings knew he was a ham, he wanted to hog up all of the media attention to himself. Trump actually had the balls to call The Pope to ask him if he could stand next to him while they did the major announcement and introduction of the new Pope. The Pope was diplomatic and told Trump via phone "hijo mío, eso no es possible."

Trump was enraged but he figured that he would still attend since he wanted to eat some free Spumoni and the occasion would offer a good opportunity to meet with the major Italian crime families to cut some lucrative deals for the Trump family. He wanted the Irish, Scottish, and Italian mobs to work together.

The Pope stepped out into the balcony; millions of people roared in joy. The Pope was dressed magnificently elegant. He waved at the crowd and spoke for five minutes in Latin. He finally got to the point and said, "this is the moment that you have been waiting for all of your life — let me present to you our new Pope — POPE LA SIGUANABA."

Thousands of people fainted once they heard the news. They could not believe what they were hearing and seeing.

La Siguanaba stepped onto the balcony holding a star sparkling flame and a tight, red, silk dress, with golden stripes. Of course, she put on a robe on top to cover her voluptuous, magnificent figure.

CHAPTER 11

S
he looked marvelous. To open her speech, they played *The Lady in Red* song by Chris De Burgh. The crowd all sang together, and The Pope began to weep. The song reminded him of the girlfriend he left behind in Poland. Once the song ended, La Siguanaba began her speech.

The crowd was mesmerized. Her voice hypnotized them. Her beauty created gasps worldwide.

She decided to give her speech in Italian, Arabian, French, Spanish, Armenian, and English. She was so audacious that she decided to wear a star of David as a necklace and to send a message of tolerance and unity among Christian, Jews, and Muslims.

She invoked the spirits of Mother Theresa, Saint Oscar Romero, Gandhi, and she dedicated her speech to Mary Magdalene, and she announced that her first executive order would be to nominate Mary Magdalene as a Saint. She was not messing around.

In her speech, she shocked the world by stating that the Catholic Church would auction half of its accumulated gold. The money raised through the auction would be used to build more churches and schools throughout the world that would teach tolerance, respect, love, and social justice. The crowds roared in approval.

She said "¿Yo soy la Papa del Pueblo, y que?"

Once she finished her speech Jorge Ramos was waiting to interview her via UNIVISION live satellites and the first question

Jorge Ramos asked her was "how do you feel to be the first female selected Pope of the Catholic Church?" La Siguanaba said "It is an honor and I will make radical, revolutionary changes that will now allow women to become priest. I will allow male priests to get married to women or other men if they choose to. ¿Y por qué no?"

Jorge Ramos asked the second question, "¿piensa usted. que la pueden asesinar?" La Siguanaba said "me vale verga." Jorge Ramos exploded in laughter and said "now that is my kind of Pope — chingona." They bonded and broke open a bottle of tequila to celebrate.

El Cadejo was livid. He wanted all of the gold for himself. But La Siguanaba was more astute than that asshole.

She had already obtained the exorcism manual from the Pope that had been kept in secret vaults for centuries. It was a wonderful potion that included ingredients that had to be grown and imported from El Salvador — the fruits to conduct the exorcism were the ingredients included in a classic *ponche*. The secret powders to also be included were *polvo de huiste* and *urine* from La Siguanaba — La Papa. Simply put, she had to do a sopa de calzon (atravez de un ponche) that included these ingredients. She bought the underwear at Victoria's Secrets close out sale. The potion from the Catholic Church would take the evil spirits out of El Cadejo and would leave him mortal, powerless, and half baboso. He would become known as El Gran Baboso and people would begin to refer to him as "el maitro baboso."

She tricked El Cadejo by inviting him to a private dinner at the Vatican promising that she would turn over half of the gold to him.

El Cadejo decided to dress up as Cristobal Colon. He wanted to make a point that he was proud of his Italian/Spanish influence. He thought that he would eat a succulent dinner of lasagna and some Spumoni.

Instead, La Siguanaba offered salpicon, nuegados con chilate, y pinche ponche. El Cadejo was sick and tired of Salvi food. He wanted only Italian and French cuisine. Pope Siguanaba welcomed El Cadejo as royalty. Her plan was similar to Jesus Christ's Last Supper and she was Judas. As soon as El Cadejo walked in, she hugged and gave El Cadejo two kisses. She told him, "we can talk business after dinner, my son." This scenario reminded her of when Archbishop Romero was set up by his own internal enemies to be murdered. She knew the true plotters and intellectual assassins who gave the orders. Roberto d'Aubuisson Arrieta was just a patsy who was used by the true decision makers and leaders of the death squads. The plot to place the sole blame on d'Aubuisson worked perfectly. The true murderers and trigger man continue to roam freely. In fact, and ironically, the trigger man now obtains free medical services at Clinica Monseor Romero in Los Angeles and has obtained Temporary Protective Status (TPS) from El Rescate for a $200 donation. He now attends Catholic mass every Sunday at Placita Olvera and he begs and prays for forgiveness to Saint Romero.

As soon as El Cadejo sat down to eat — he finished the salpicón, nuegados con chilate, y se tomó el ponche. As soon as he finished el ponche, he began to speak in tongues and powder began to burst out of his mouth — they were the evil spirits that had invaded and taken over his body for centuries.

¡La Siguanaba burst into uncontrollable laughter and told El Cadejo, "ahora si te jodiste hijo de la gran puta!"

"I am now the Pope motherfucker and you are now fucked," continued La Siguanaba. "You just drank El Ponche that has a secret recipe to expel your supernatural demon powers. Now I will roast your meat to make tacos and pupusas revueltas."

El Cadejo was shocked that his supernatural powers and immortality were now gone.

La Siguanaba called the head chef of El Vaticano, along

with her bodyguards, and ordered for El Cadejo to be taken away — to be prepared into meat for tacos and pupusas.

El Cadejo cried and cried and asked for forgiveness to La Siguanaba and he reminded her that they had two son's together: El Cipitio and El Duende. La Siguanaba/The Pope could not be moved nor convinced.

She said "ojo por ojo, diente por diente. Take this piece of shit away and place him in the mental hospital holding area before we cook his ass," she shouted.

Now La Papa (La Siguanaba) could focus on beginning her work and implementation of her leadership skills as the new Pope.

She was not fucking around. If anyone would dare question her authority, La Siguanaba would simply resort to her gangster roots by saying "what the fuck?" and then anyone would get intimidated and back off. She may have left her home country, el Mercado, and the ghetto, but she kept her hood credentials. She wanted to keep it real even though she was officially La Papa.

First, she would impose a new law of "ojo por ojo, diente por diente" since she believed in the Old Testament. She would order her secret service of the The Vatican to chop off the penis of any pedophile priest.

Then, she would pass religious mandates that would also punish public school district abusers and Boy Scout employees who would abuse Boy Scout and Girl Scout children. She would become the Genghis Khan of Popes. She passed a mandate of boiling abusers alive. The Catholic Church was shocked but had no choice but to agree to the new Pope mandates.

Pope Siguanaba became the cruelest Pope ever with criminals. She would say "fuck that biblical shit about forgiveness. Forgive criminals? Oh fuck no!"

Crime rates in Catholic majority countries plummeted. The criminals and abusers of women and children panicked when they simply heard Pope Siguanaba's name.

They would tell each other "esa vieja te manda a cortar la verga y si se enoja — te cocina como cangrejo – en agua hirviendo."

Finally, the world had a leader that was not portrayed as a benevolent saint. Pope Siguanaba wanted to be perceived as a chingona with no aspirations of being canonized or made into a Saint.

She also legalized same sex marriage — even among the clergy. Fuck, the priest and archbishops got diarrhea for many weeks due to her decisions. Others were so ecstatic and happy that they no longer had to hide their sexual orientation. They could be free to express to the world that they were gay or bisexual.

While El Cadejo was being held in the Vatican deviant prison, he escaped. The motherfucker was still a genius when it came to plots and ploys. He returned to El Salvador - to Izalco, to find the oldest brujo who could once again blend a potion that would give him his magical and evil powers back. Immortality, able to take on different body and animal shapes, and supernatural strength.

Pope Siguanaba was livid that he escaped but she figured that she was well protected within The Vatican secret security forces.

Now, La Siguanaba had to reign with an iron first, yet with a willingness to share and spread love to all. She would continue to implement the teachings of Jesus Christ, but she was also pragmatic.

Her next steps in life were to see if she could reconcile with her two sons: El Cipitio and El Duende. It would take a miracle, but she was willing to wait and try.

She would need to make up her abandonment of her two sons. She hated the word charity since she believed in helping others, but more powerfully, in other's helping themselves. Pope Siguanaba's message included self-empowerment. She was tired of people whining and complaining. She wanted people to shift their mindset from victimhood to sisterhood and brotherhood. She began to sound like Mother Teresa of Calcutta.

She led by example by visiting the sick people in hospitals and even broke bread with people that had terminal illnesses. She wanted to give them hope and strength. She volunteered at drug and alcohol rehabilitation centers since she knew many were scams that only wanted to get the Obamacare/L.A. Care funding. She was also aware that many of the non-profits set up to help the addicts, homeless, and gangsters were set up to mainly fund the fat salaries of the fat cats getting rich off the suffering of the poor. She wanted to help the poor directly — with no salary. She would say "billions of dollars have been allocated and invested to help reduce drug/alcohol addiction, gang affiliations, homelessness, but has that money helped reduce these problems, and who is getting the money anyway?

Slowly, Pope Siguanaba started to take on Princess Diana's and Dolores Huerta's social justice work and role. People began to refer to Pope Siguanaba as the Pope of the People. La Papa de la gente. Pope Siguanaba wanted to use the wealth and influence of the Catholic Church to do good. She wanted to take the Catholic Church back to its original roots, which was to help the poor.

She held a major speech at the Vatican and she admitted to the atrocities of the Catholic Church's colonization and building of missions throughout North and South America. She admitted that the indigenous populations were plundered and that their cultural roots, language, and traditions were uprooted.

Pope Siguanaba admitted the injustices and apologized. The world was in awe of her natural beauty, intelligence, and sincerity. She was no longer the usual Pope. She was La Papa del Pueblo.

Pope Siguanaba had everything she wanted in life, except

the love of her two sons. The guilt tortured her, but she was going to do everything in her power to develop trust and to seek the recognition and love from her two abandoned children from long ago.

She wanted more people to know about postpartum depression so that why she committed such a so-called crime could be better understood. She even hired Christy Turlington to do a PSA describing the struggles of women when giving birth and to shed more light on the issue of postpartum depression. They became natural allies and buddies.

She also asked Elton John to write and sign a song regarding these topics, creating duets with Adele, Lady Gaga, and Cardi B.

The song that Elton John created was better and more emotionally moving than *Candle in the Wind.* All of the profits gained from the song were donated to The Postpartum Depression Awareness non-profit.

Elton John whispered into Pope Siguanaba's ear and gave her an excellent idea. "Why don't you create a concert, with special guest the Electric Light Orchestra, and they can sing Telephone Line dedicated to El Cipitio and El Duende? I will invite them to be my special guests and you can come meet them in my special, private suite."

Pope Siguanaba was in awe. She responded by saying "perfecto."

The concert would take place at Wembley Stadium in London, England.

Elton John made sure that it would be the most magnificent concert to honor Pope Siguanaba and to help reconcile El Cipitio and El Duende with Pope Siguanaba.

The lighting and sound system was incredible. The Electric Light Orchestra was truly excited to play for Pope Siguanaba. It was an honor for them.

Pope Siguanaba sat in a private suite to view and listen to

the concert. Once it was over, Elton John would bring El Cipitio and El Duende to visit their estranged mother.

They had no clue that the purpose of the concert was to reunite them and for Pope Siguanaba to make two major announcements: she would create two immediate executive orders. One allowing priests to marry and the second was a bomb shell: to legalize abortion! Pope Siguanaba knew that a split would occur within the Catholic Church and that recall efforts would be made to get rid of her. She did not give a fuck. She wanted women to decide for themselves and not men. She gave a thunderous speech and made the two announcements. The crowd was mesmerized by her beauty, intelligence and shocking announcements. They gasped when she announced that she would make abortion legal and ended her remarks by saying "y que hueyes?"

El Cipitio and El Duende truly enjoyed the concert and they were so entranced by the Pope's shocking announcements but they both agreed that the church needed to change and accept abortions.

Once the speeches and concerts were over, Elton John, told them "I have special surprise for both of you." El Cipitio and El Duende smiled.

CHAPTER 12

A s they walked into the magnificent VIP suite, Pope Siguanaba stood up and both, El Cipitio and El Duende were taken aback to see their mother as Pope Siguanaba, in all of her splendor. They did not know that they were going to see her in person, in private.

She broke the ice by saying "hola hijitos, aqui está su madre y les pido disculpas por haberlos ahogados en el rio y con mis tetotas. Especialmente le pido perdón a Ud. El Cipitio porque no lo quería por nacer negrito, panzon, y por tener los pies al revez. Aquí le tengo unos guineos majonchitos para su estomaguito."

El Cipitio and El Duente were angry but Elton John had a surprise. He began to sing to *Candle in the Wind* just for Pope Siguanaba and El Cipitio and El Duende. All of a sudden, El Cipitio and El Duende began to sing along with Elton John. A miracle was taking place.

After the song, Pope Siguanaba asked El Cipitio and El Duende for forgiveness. She said, "my two sons, I beg for your forgiveness. What I did has no excuse, but I was going through postpartum depression." El Cipitio said, "oh yes, I saw the PSA done by Christy Turlington and I understand better."

El Duende interjected and said, "si, ahora entendemos lo que le pasaba Papa Siguanaba, mejor dicho, Mama Siguanaba."

Pope Siguanaba started to cry out of joy. She could not believe that her two sons had finally forgiven her. Pope Siguanaba's prayers finally came true.

Now, she could be at peace and the guilt and shame could no longer control her.

She asked the sound engineers from the concert to blast *No Debes Jugar* by Selena. She said, "I am the Pope but does not mean that I cannot get down to Selenas." She also requested Cuco's best hits to be played for El Cipitio and El Duende. The DJ blasted the *Bossa no sé* song. El Cipitio and El Duende loved it! Once they played the songs *Lo que siento* and *Drown* by Cuco and Clairo they began to super trip.

The sound engineers also decided to throw in Careless Whisper by George Michael to honor his memory.

La Siguanaba, El Cipitio, El Duende, and Elton John sang the song together and cried while they held each other tight, without letting go:

I'm never gonna dance again
Guilty feet have got no rhythm
Though it's easy to pretend
I know you're not a fool
I should've known better than to cheat a friend
And waste the chance that I've been given
So I'm never gonna dance again
The way I danced with you

El Cadejo roamed and hid within the volcanoes of El Salvador. He no longer had immortality or supernatural strength. He would hunt garrobos with an hondilla and he would boil the garrobos/iguanas in hot boiling water. He wanted to overcome his erectile dysfunction but the sopa de garrobo was of no help! la palomita ya no se le paraba.

The only possession he had in life was an old tape, battery powered radio player from the 1980s that he used to listen to music. He had to attach a CD player to listen to CDs. He got all soft and sentimental when he played Luis Miguel's *Culpable o no*.

Then he decided to take a heroin hit while he blasted *Intocable* and *Bronco's* best hits. His mind took him back to the past. He was now an old and lonely, broken demon. He began to cry when Intocable's *Tu Eres Mi Droga* and *Enséñame a Olvidar* played. Then he blasted Bronco's *Oro* song and he cried with great pain. He had to admit that he missed La Siguanaba, El Cipitio, and El Duende. He dedicated the *Oro* song to La Siguanaba as a goodbye. He cried and cried and began to sing with extreme sadness along with Guadalupe Esparza's voice:

Nunca oí consejos y me enamoré
Yo al ras del suelo
Y tú siempre volando tan alto, tan alto
Te gusta el dinero y la comodidad
Por eso me dejas muy triste
Y herido de muerte, que suerte
Oro
Tu me has cambiado por oro
Te has olvidado de lo sentimental
Por un puñado de metal
Oro
El amarillo del oro
'Te gustó más de lo que yo te ofrecí
Y ahora tú te vas de mí
Oro
El oro cambió tu amor
Yo te regalé una luna sin miel
Una cama blanda y
Una almohada repleta de sueños
Pequeños
Tal vez no bastó con lo que tengo aquí
Y tu amor su fue por el hoyo
Que hay en mis bolsillos, vacíos